Shortlisted for the Blue Peter 'Book I Couldn't Put Down' Award

'Johnson's writing is witty and inventive, and the character of Thora ... is full of unexpectedness ... This is a book full of fun.' *Sunday Times* children's book of the week

'Thora is an irresistible character with an attitude that's all her own! Though modern in its telling, this tale has a timeless feel to it – storytelling at its best.' Starred review, *Publishing News*

'An attractively illustrated and uplifting story.' *Times Educational Supplement*

More books about everyone's
favourite half-mermaid:

Thora
Thora and the Green Sea-Unicorn

Thora

and the Incredible Crystals

written and illustrated by
Gillian Johnson

a division of Hachette Children's Books

First published by HarperCollins Publishers,
Sydney, Australia, in 2007.
This edition published by arrangement with
HarperCollins Publishers Pty Limited.
This edition published in Great Britain in 2007
by Hodder Children's Books

1

A Catalogue record for this book is available
from the British Library

ISBN-13: 978 0 340 88446 1

Printed and bound in Great Britain by
Clays Ltd, St Ives plc

The paper and board used in this paperback by Hodder
Children's Books are natural recyclable products made from
wood grown in sustainable forests. The manufacturing
processes conform to the environmental regulations of the
country of origin.

Hodder Children's Books
A division of Hachette Children's Books
338 Euston Road, London NW1 3BH
An Hachette Livre UK Company

for Jannie, Pin + Toady

Prologue

One hot, blue, windy afternoon, a cruise ship docked in a small bay at Gun Carriage Island off the north-east coast of Tasmania.

A tiny woman and her tinier dog disembarked and blinked into the bright sun. The woman wore her hair scraped back into a tight black knot. Her bun was the size of an olive and held in place by two red chopsticks. Her jacket and trousers were crisp, but plain, her legs were bowed and her feet bare. She wore no rings on her fingers, no earrings, no make-up. It was impossible to guess her age.

The pug she set down on the beach, however, was very old.

The small dog teetered on pencil-thin legs, then balanced itself, coughed, wheezed and snorted. Its fur was short, like a seal's, and of a bristly salt-and-pepper colour that you sometimes see on the eyebrows of seafaring uncles. Its right eye protruded and oozed a sticky liquid, and its lips and tongue were grey and dry.

The hideous growths on its head, back, ears and legs were definitely not beauty spots. They were warts.

Madame Pong loved her dog very much. But now, on the shark-tooth-white sand of this windy island in Bass Strait, she intended to leave her ailing but beloved Yen-Ting forever. She had chosen this little island at the top of Tasmania as his resting place because of its extreme beauty. She had read somewhere that the Vikings sometimes laid the gravely ill in boats and pushed them out to a watery death on the sea. She did not have a boat. Not yet. Rather, she would leave her dog on the beach of the most beautiful island in the world.

To die.

With a heavy heart, Madame Pong reached into her pocket for a farewell pork dumpling.

Madame Pong was a cunning businesswoman. She was as famous for her thriftiness as she was for Pong's Pools, the name of her thriving healing spa company in Taipei.

Madame Pong had inherited the business from her father, Professor Pi Pong. Pong's Pools offered alternative therapy to people who believed that crystals and gemstones had the power to cure their every ailment – headaches, allergies, knee pain, heart problems, eczema, halitosis, nerves, night terrors, bedwetting, insomnia, pimples, warts, obesity, excessive hairiness, sadness, giggles, bad moods, temper tantrums and smelly armpits.

Wealthy clients came from all over the world to soak in the luxury baths and have their energy flows realigned using rose quartz, jasper, topaz and lapis lazuli, to name just a few. But where Professor P. Pong had been a cuddly philanthropist with a dimple in his left cheek and a shy, playful manner, his daughter was strictly business. She did not give money away; she made it. And with a pug dog as her only family, her fortune grew.

Madame Pong was as mean with herself as she was with her staff. Her house was small. She slept on the floor on a single green futon in an unheated room. She spent as little money and time as possible on clothes, adopting a peasant look that was as severe and unvarying as a school uniform. Madame Pong had studied physics and mathematics at university. She was a scientist. She saw the world in black and white – yes or no, plus or minus. And maybe because of this she was a little impatient with the mysteries of crystals. It was impossible for Madame Pong to explain scientifically to herself or to others how exactly the crystals *worked*. But she didn't have to. Her marketing department did that for her. And the clients paid well.

Though she didn't really believe in crystals, she believed wholeheartedly in her dog. When it came to Yen-Ting, Madame Pong was an extravagant mush-bucket.

Nothing gave Madame Pong more intense pleasure than to dress Ting up in one of his sparkly silver coats and escort him out to dinner in downtown Taipei. For years they dined together twice a week at the well-known Dai Tin Heng on Koo Yi Road. Even after the tourists ruined the atmosphere of the place, she retained her reserved seating and so never had to wait very long.

As Ting grew older and developed breathing problems, Madame Pong created a face-mask to prevent him from inhaling the car fumes and polluted city air. Pugs are sensitive to the heat and so on warm nights

Madame Pong attached a clip-on fan to the edge of his carry basket so that he could stay cool while she hand-fed him cuttlefish chips, *otah*, and his favourite: fragrant rice cooked in coconut milk. Tourists would marvel at the sight of this peasant-dressed woman feeding her dog *xiao long bao* (steamed pork dumplings). They snapped Ting's photograph. They whispered and pointed. Madame Pong took no notice.

As Ting aged, he was struck down with further health problems.

He began to shed his coat. Black hairs appeared everywhere in Madame Pong's house. They floated up into her rice, her clothes, her small flared nostrils. Once she even found three of Ting's hairs in the bristles of her toothbrush.

Always a snorter, he started to wake Madame Pong up in the middle of the night with odd, pig-like noises.

His coughing spells frightened her.

Several times she thought he was choking to death.

Over the years, she had put aside her doubts and tried dozens of different crystals to realign Ting's chakras: citrines, bloodstones, garnets, tourmalines, rubies, amethysts. When the crystals did not work, she tried acupuncture, homeopathy, Reiki, colour therapy, cranio-sacral therapy, aromatherapy. A change in diet and three operations on Ting's nose and throat did little to improve his breathing difficulties.

He developed mange. Grew allergic to chilli.

Sometimes he foamed at the mouth.

He had seizures.

At his sixteenth birthday party, over a bowl of *xiao long bao*, Ting's bulgy eyes turned cloudy and began to run into his soup. The next morning Madame Pong found Ting lying on his futon like a marooned dumpling.

He survived, but Madame Pong realised that her pug dog's time was running out. It was not fair to keep the poor beast alive. He had not smiled in over a year. And the worst of it, he needed nappies.

Madame Pong had planned Ting's death carefully.

The luxury cruise ship, the exquisite sandy beach on the most distant island in the world, the final pork dumpling – which she produced now from a jacket pocket and offered to her sick dog.

'Here, Tingy! The ship's cook prepared it especially for you: *xiao long bao*!'

Yen-Ting glared at the steamed dumpling, dropped his head and began chewing the sand at his feet.

'But it's your *favourite*!'

Then she noticed something sparkly in Ting's mouth.

'Drop it!' she ordered.

Ting refused. The small, hard object made a gritty sound as he chewed on it.

She reached down and tried to open his mouth. 'Give it to me!' she yelled.

Ting swallowed and closed his eyes.

Madame Pong felt faint. 'Ting! Ting! Are you dead?'

Ting stood very still for what seemed like three days but what in fact was less than a minute.

Then he opened his eyes and threw Madame Pong a look so bright that she reached for her sunglasses.

His tail began to wag.

The goo that had been dripping from his right eye dried up. His nose turned black, his lips moist, his eyes curious.

She watched in astonishment as one by one the hideous warts on his back disappeared.

POP! POP! POP!

Ting then stood up on his hind legs and turned in a circle. Pugs don't bark, but they smile, and a grin

spread from ear to ear across Ting's lovable squashed face.

With a playful yap, he ripped off his dog nappy and scampered toward the dunes.

Madame Pong sprinted after him, her bare feet churning the sand, her chopsticks clicking. 'Ting! Ting! Come back!'

In the hour that followed, Madame Pong became a believer.

Her trouser pockets bursting with small, sparkly objects, Madame Pong returned home to Taipei after a brief stop in Hobart.

The staff at Pong's Pools were surprised when their boss came to work with a puppy pug named Ting. Had she really replaced her old dog so quickly? Some felt it was a little insensitive. Of course, nobody said a word.

Madame Pong did not provide an explanation.

Nor did she elaborate on where or how she had discovered the crystals that she submitted to the resident scientists for analysis.

She was concerned about Yen-Ting's substantial hair-loss. But otherwise, he was fine. Happy and healthy, with the energy of a small pup.

The results from the lab were exciting. The stones were definitely crystals. They had the structural complexity of diamonds and unusually powerful vibrational energies.

Madame Pong herself began to hum with what in the world of alternative healing is called 'a positive energy'. Someone saw her smile. Another claimed to have heard her laugh. There were whispers about a spring in her step.

But the effects of the crystals were not confined to Madame Pong. The healers and the healed alike emerged from the labs and treatment rooms wearing blissed-out grins. Everyone was rapturous about the effects of the highly secret new ingredients in Pong's Pools.

'This morning I woke with my usual dreadful, pounding, throbbing headache. A soak in the pools sorted out my chakras almost instantly. I feel fantastic now.'

'I have always suffered from allergies that give me wet, raw rashes on my scalp, on my elbows and behind my knees. My rashes are really painful and they develop smelly yellow crusts that make it hard for me to attract the girls. After three sessions in the pools I am a new man! I'm going out on a date tonight! Wish me luck!'

'My son stopped wetting his bed after one session in Madame Pong's pools. Thank you, lady!'

'I am a grandparent, but I now feel like a teenager!'

Sworn to silence, the staff were soon referring to the sparkly objects (amongst themselves) as Incredible Crystals.

A meeting was held at which Madame Pong announced her vision. 'As you know, the crystals that I have discovered could turn this company into the most successful healing centre in the world. I am happy to announce that we will now be entering the export business.' She paused. 'I have produced a design for Exportable Crystal-Encrusted Spa Baths and Pools.

Clients need only fill their tubs with water and climb in, to experience the crystals' magical healing powers. We will continue to run our healing centre and scientific laboratory right here in Taipei. But we will also *sell* our spa baths and pools to sultans, kings, queens, movie stars, football players, IT magnates and Russian oligarchs. (In other words, filthy rich people who want to extend their lives, feel youthful and look like a million bucks.)

'We will *clean up* in the world of private spa baths. Jacuzzis will be regarded as the dinosaurs of an ancient and unenlightened time!

'Each bath requires at least fifty crystals. So we will need many, many, *many* more crystals. As far as I know, the only place in the world where these crystals exist in great quantities is *Gun Carriage Island* off the north-east coast of Tasmania, Australia.'

She stopped for a breath and pointed to a map.

'Your task is to work out how we will bring the stones from Australia into Taiwan. I want a full report: research plan, exportation procedure and costing. Get me a budget. Now, go.'

Three weeks later, Madame Pong received the results of the feasibility study. That afternoon an emergency meeting was held.

With the report in her hand, Madame Pong stepped up on to a wooden stool and called out: 'ATTENTION, EVERYONE, QUIET!'

She needn't have told them that, because nobody was saying anything.

Madame Pong's anger was a tsunami – silencing those before it, drowning everything in its wake.

She pulled one of the chopsticks out of her bun and jabbed it at the report lying on the table in front of her. Thin black strands of hair hung over her face and gave her a wild look. She read:

'The Australian Government does not permit the export of precious stones or minerals from its country. Recommendation: manufacture an imitation using synthetic ingredients.'

She threw the report up into the air.

Everyone watched the pages drift to the floor.

Madame Pong whipped out the other chopstick and clacked them together. 'Imitation?'

Silence.

'You recommend we *manufacture*' – she narrowed her eyes and repeated the key words of the report – 'an *imitation* product using *synthetic* ingredients.' She paused significantly. 'Is that the best you can do?'

'Synthetic is the new natural?' ventured one brave employee.

'It is pathetic,' she said, stabbing the air with her chopsticks. 'You are all *pathetic*.' She pointed a chopstick

at each of the workers. 'YOU! YOU! YOU! YOU! YOU! And yes, YOU!'

Suddenly, she used her chopsticks to produce a drum roll on the table, tossed her head and hair and smiled in a way that was often compared (behind her back) to the squashed smile of her pug dog Yen-Ting – though it was much rarer.

'Leave it to me,' she said, laughing, which was rarer still. The sound that came out of her mouth sounded a little like *teeeeeheeeeeheeee*.

✯

As another busy day gave way to evening shadow, Madame Pong sat cross-legged on her futon studying the white business card that she had been given by a heavily perfumed old lady in a café in Hobart. She had met the woman and her husband shortly after her remarkable adventure with Ting on the beach at Gun Carriage Island. The couple were childless and had run a toy shop in Salamanca Market for many years, selling remote-control fire-engines, wind-up platypuses, stuffed wombats, marbles, chewing gum and toy cricket sets.

Madame Pong recalled the woman's watery eyes, bleached to the colour of weak green tea by sun, advancing years and life's disappointments.

Madame Pong straightened her chopsticks and picked up the phone.

'Hello, Mrs Ferguson?' she began. 'It's Madame Pong calling you from Taipei. We met last month at the café at Salamanca Market. Yes, I was the person with the puppy. He's well, thank you. Very well indeed. Now tell me . . . just how *badly* do you want a child?'

Seven years later ...

chapter 1

'Mother?'

No answer.

'Mr Walters?'

No answer.

'Cosmo?'

Nothing.

Where *was* everybody? Still sleeping? What a pile of slugabeds! Lazybones! Waste trails!

It was almost 9 a.m. and Thora had just sighted Australia!

Holding the binoculars, she leaped down off the roof of the *Loki* – where she shouldn't have been sitting anyway, for many of the houseboat's shingles had come loose on their journey. Her windsurfing slippers made a satisfying *smuch* as she landed on the deck. She brushed a strand of hair out of her eyes and made a quick adjustment to her ponytail, a fountain spray of conker-brown hair tied on the top of her head to hide her blow hole.

'M-o-th-er!'

After four months at sea, Thora was itchy to feel land under her windsurfing slippers once more. Through the binoculars she could see the thirty-metre dolerite cliffs near Port Arthur. 'Just what the convictions would've seen two hundred years ago as they sailed towards Van Demonised Land!' she thought.

She went inside the cabin, letting the screen door bang shut behind her. In the living room, she drew open the sliding Plexiglas cover and peered down into the pizza-shaped hole in the middle of the floor.

'Moth-er!'

This hole was Halla's 'mermaid flap', allowing her to come and go as she pleased. But she wasn't there now.

Thora sprang up and strode towards her Guardian Angle's bedroom cabin. She *smuched* her heels together and knocked.

No answer.

She opened his door. His camp bed was made up, the red wool blanket pulled army-tight, the pillow fluffed. But no Mr Walters. The grandfather clock beside the oak wardrobe read 9.03 a.m.

Where *were* they? She marched back outside.

'Cos-mo!'

Silence.

Suddenly Thora stopped. The dolerite cliffs had vanished.

'Jeepers, where's Australia gone?' she said to herself.

The *Loki* had been swallowed by a great hot stillness. A bolt of fear circled Thora's blow hole and leaped down the length of her spine, her arms, her legs. The boat was slowing. Or was it?

'This is highly illegible,' she declared. Less than five minutes before, the air had been fresh, the sea sparkling, the sun a warm, ripening orange in the sky.

Now the air felt thick, like the steam room at the skiing chalet in Spittal after Halla swam Lake Millstätter in Austria. As if it's trying to suffragette us, thought Thora.

There was an unexpected scraping sound.

Thora rushed to the stern. A frazzled-looking Mr Walters was dragging a deckchair toward Halla, who waved at her through the vapoury swirls. 'I heard you calling.' She looked relieved to see her daughter.

'What's going on?' Thora asked.

'Wish I knew,' said Mr Walters. 'I've lost the Ashes.'

'Already?' said Thora. 'But doesn't the Test last five days?'

'I mean on the radio. The reception's kaput!' He looked up at the sky. 'Really, this haze is *most* extraordinary. Pull up a chair and join us.'

Chapter 2

Though Thora had visited mainland Australia as a small girl when her mother was swimming the lakes and oceans of the world, she had never been to Tasmania.

Perhaps because of his poor health over the past year, Mr Walters had dreamed constantly of returning to Hobart, the place where he and his late wife, Imogen, had spent their honeymoon. The place where they had felt most at home on earth. Nobody had spoken about it openly, but there was a sinking sense that Mr Walters might not have a lot of time left. He was eighty-three years old and his energy was declining. For this reason, Thora and Halla were more than happy to begin their Tasmanian adventure in Hobart, the capital city. Mr Walters looked forward to sipping tea and nibbling lamingtons in the old tea rooms that dotted Battery Point. He had loved the sandstone houses, the bright harbour, the bustling Salamanca Market, the slow trail up Mount Wellington with its stories of snowy peaks in mid-summer.

After Hobart, the family would travel to Flinders Island – the small, out of the way island off the north-east coast.

Flinders was Cosmo's birthplace. Ten years had passed since the blue-necked Indian peacock was given to Halla as a prize for swimming the Bunyip River near Melbourne. The family had always promised him that one day they would take him back. All those years he must have been yearning to see his long-lost parents, aunts, uncles, cousins and friends again. And now that they were getting closer to Flinders, he had been pacing the boat in the manner of an impatient aristocrat.

The tiny population and rocky shoreline of Flinders appealed to Halla. She was tired of the prying eyes of mermaid watchers and was drawn to the guidebook's photos of orange granite boulders and quiet turquoise lagoons with their borders of eucalypts and feathery-needled she-oaks. 'It looks like a jewel of a place,' she'd said with a sigh. 'Imagine the decorating possibilities on those rocks!'

Halla had discovered her passion for exterior decorating after retiring from the swimming circuit. She had a talent for converting even the plainest rock into a luxury boulder.

'That orange lichen looks as thick as those deep-pile carpets at the Holiday Inn in Toledo,' she observed.

Thora was sure that Shirley, the other member of their family, would have loved Flinders too. But the little green sea unicorn had parted ways with the *Loki* a few months earlier near the Maldives. She was always a determined creature and had been anxious to return to her independent life. Thora missed her, although she knew that Shirley could more than take care of herself.

And how did Thora feel about Flinders?

She was always game for an adventure.

Chapter 3

The seas around Tasmania were known to be a bit wild. The little family on the *Loki* had been expecting some challenges and they were well-prepared. Sailing the big oceans came as naturally to Thora as doing cartwheels and was as satisfying to Mr Walters as listening to the cricket commentary.

Now on the brink of entering Storm Bay to begin their final leg to Hobart, they suddenly found themselves stopped short.

The water spread flat in every direction. 'It's not just the radio that's affected,' said Mr Walters. 'The motor has cut out. The transmitter's down too. It's a total dead zone.'

'Could it be the doldrums?' asked Thora, thinking of the hot, heavy days near the Cocos Islands, where the boat had listed aimlessly for a spell.

'No,' said Mr Walters. His knees cracked and he sat down in his chair with a stack of charts balancing on his bony thighs. 'Wrong place. Wrong time of year. It's something else – though I don't know what.

Something irregular. Mysterious.' He reached into his pocket for a cigar, a sign that something was awry. He usually only smoked after sundown.

'It's as if there's been an organic disaster,' observed Thora. 'An underwater volcanic elliption or something!'

'Perhaps.' Mr Walters frowned. 'But I should think a volcano would stir up the sea – not calm it.' He glanced down at the flat water. 'Listen to that silence. *Most* peculiar.' He crossed one long leg over another and lit his cigar.

'And no birds,' added Halla. 'Not even a gull.'

'And where is that dweezly old albatross that's been following us?' asked Thora, head tilted back to look at the sky. 'And the dolphins I saw a few kilometres back!'

Cosmo coughed and looked away. He hated cigar smoke.

'Tell me,' said Mr Walters, turning to face Thora, 'does the projectionist's ring still work?'

She touched the gold band that dangled from a chain around her neck. 'It feels a little warm, actually.'

The ring grew warm only during times of great significance. At least, that had been the pattern so far.

'Could you test it, Thora?' asked Halla.

The projectionist's ring came from the Allbent Cinema in Grimli-By-The-Sea. Thora's grandmother had intended the magic ring for Halla's wedding present. That was before Halla's husband, Thora's father, had disappeared.

Thora removed the ring from around her neck and went inside. Simply by slipping the ring on to the base of Mr Walters' ancient sixteen-millimetre projector, Thora had been able to watch an endless variety of classic films. On their previous ocean journey, the family had spent many hours sprawled on the floor of Thora's bedroom munching popcorn and marvelling at the stories that unfolded on the ceiling.

But now the images overhead swirled and melted, like the sugar and butter mixtures in the fudge that Thora often made on the *Loki*'s stovetop.

Shaking her head, she went back to join the others on deck.

In the few minutes that she had been inside, the hazy stillness had wrapped itself around the boat like gauze. The heat pressed down, thick and suffocating.

In his white trousers and vest, Mr Walters resembled a tall, elongated ghost.

'The ring isn't working properly,' she said to him. 'The images are all wonky.'

'Is the ring still warm?' wondered Mr Walters.

Thora nodded. 'Where is Mother?'

Mr Walters pointed. 'In the water.'

Being a mermaid, Halla never spent too much time on deck, as her tail tended to dry out.

'I asked her not to get in,' Mr Walters added. 'But she said the sea was calling her.'

'*Calling* her?' Thora leaned over the railing, relieved to see Halla's tail close to the surface. 'Mother, what do you mean when you say the water is "calling" you? What's it saying?'

'I don't quite understand it,' Halla said, a little dreamily, 'but I feel a force of some kind, something almost, well, magnetic! Not entirely unpleasant, either.' Her tail gleamed in the cloud-coloured water. She looked somehow lit from within.

'Have you seen anything?' asked Thora.

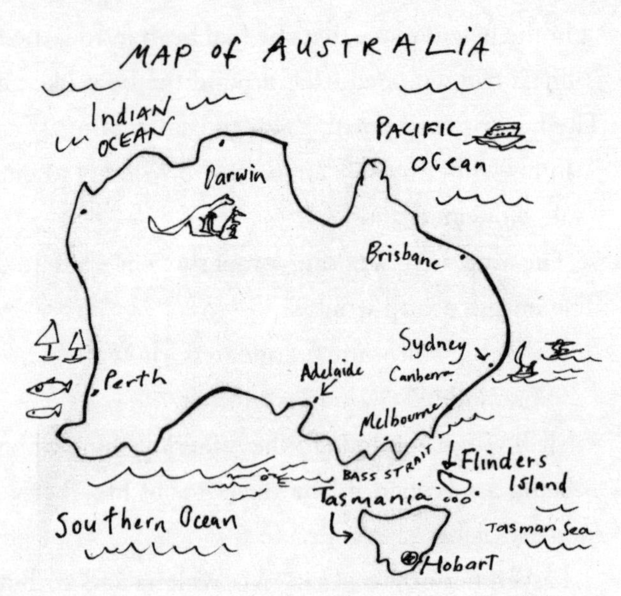

'Nothing. There is nothing in the water. *At all.* It's as if the ocean has been evacuated. I have never known it like this.'

'Maybe it's because we're in Australia,' said Thora, 'where everything is upside down. Topsy-turvoid.'

Halla considered. 'Whatever, it's weird. It's as if we've been bewitched. Or Sea-Shrewed.'

Cosmo shivered.

'Halla, *pleease* be a sensible mermaid,' said Mr Walters forcefully, 'and come on board this minute.'

Cosmo cocked his head as though in agreement, his eyes shining like two black worry beads under his head crest.

The haze did not lift that day.

chapter 4

Adelaide Ferguson found a fax in her machine when she arrived at her office at The Deep Breath Hotel & Spa on Monday morning at 7 a.m.

> I WILL RING AT 8 TO DISCUSS AN URGENT MATTER. MADAME PONG.

Heart quickening, Adelaide prepared for the call. What could Madame Pong want?

Madame Pong's new cruise ship, the *Yen-Ting*, had left Melbourne the night before and was scheduled to arrive at Flinders Island by ten o'clock. Sixty-one guests would be descending on The Deep Breath Hotel, sixty-one demanding individuals who expected to be seriously pampered.

This influx from Asia occurred twelve times a year. Adelaide was an old pro: everything was ready for them. Nevertheless, the terse fax worried her.

Adelaide turned in her swivel chair to sharpen her pencil over the rubbish bin, fluttering her free fingers to avoid chipping her nail polish. Adelaide was a careful dresser, with an eye for detail. To ward off the morning chill, she wore a twin set of soft pink cashmere with mother-of-pearl buttons, and crisp black Capri trousers. On her feet, a pair of white lace-up buckskin shoes – practical for all the running about she would be doing that day – and behind her ears, two tiny dabs of Blue Waltz perfume: a present from her husband, Bruce, many, many, many years before.

She blew on the sharpener to free the final shavings, and opened a red file marked HOTEL. She tapped her pencil on the desk as her eyes scrolled down the first page of the highly confidential Guest Register. It contained the names, contact numbers, professional status, ages, and many more personal details, such as allergies, hobbies, hopes and fears, of Madame Pong's hand-selected clients.

She scanned the file of Mrs Cho: a fifty-eight-year-old former model, allergic to all dairy, wheat and aubergine products, seeking to regain a flatter tummy and slimmer thighs. A typical profile. Adelaide slotted her into Room 12.

Adelaide was pleased. The group arriving today included two old Taiwanese movie stars, a Singaporean opera singer, a plastic-bag manufacturer from Madagascar, a Hong Kong perfumier who owned an English football club, a gymnast who'd won a gold medal on the balance beam at the 1968 Olympics and at least a dozen 'former models'. Meeting new people was the best part of the job, especially when they were a bit glamorous – though in reality they were all very self-centred and demanding.

After assigning each guest a room, Adelaide fiddled with one of her crystal pendant earrings and opened another file to address more mundane matters.

The guest and treatment rooms had been cleaned and were in immaculate order.

The yoga mats had been sanitised and aired.

All she needed to do was switch on the pool heaters and bring in the final load of towels from the laundry.

The pools were the heart of the business. They had been designed six years ago by Madame Pong herself. They resembled large, glittering baths and measured two metres by one metre. Though they were installed in the homes of exceedingly rich people all over the world, The Deep Breath Hotel was the only place outside of Pong's Pools in Taipei to boast as many as twenty baths in a single location.

She moved on down the sheet.

The lawn had been cut.

The sprinkler system should turn on automatically at 8 a.m. She'd had problems with it the day before and made a note to speak to Trevor, who doubled as her 'water expert'.

The pool cleaner would arrive at 9 a.m.

Fresh organic fruit and veg would arrive at 8.30 a.m. Bread at 8.45 a.m. Lentils and pulses at nine o'clock. The kitchen staff would also arrive at nine to prepare the welcoming lunch for the guests: abalone, miso soup, salad, vegetarian lasagne, tofu and bean risotto, and a selection of fresh fruit, freshly squeezed juices and fruit yogurts.

Adelaide set the file aside and reached for the blue file marked EEKOBEASTIES INC. on the shelf above her desk.

Chapter 5

The times in between the boatloads of international guests could be slow. Very few Australians stayed at The Deep Breath Hotel. Adelaide worked herself to the bone with Eekobeasties during these 'off times'.

Eekobeasties Inc. was a toy factory that produced Squidgy Dinosaurs using natural, local materials. Only handfuls of the dinosaurs were sold on Flinders itself; the beautiful island was off the beaten track and few tourists visited. But it was in the Asian market that the toys had really taken off. Children, especially small boys, loved them.

Why? Adelaide put their success down to their indestructibility. The iridescent blue-green creatures could be pulled, stretched, bounced, stomped on – but no matter how much you poked, prodded and squeezed they *always retained their shape.*

Their success abroad had been a surprise to everyone, especially Madame Pong, who saw herself as a scientist, not a toy maker. The brisk sales had made Eekobeasties

almost as lucrative as Pong's Pools. They had sent Madame Pong to the top of the World's Richest Green Women list. And the 'eco' label had ensured her moral standing in the business community.

While Adelaide ran the business side of things from her office at the hotel, the factory and warehouse were located in the local township of Blackie's Bother, and were run by Adelaide's left-handed right-hand woman, Viv Wheely. Thank goodness for Viv – who also baby-sat Adelaide's daughter, Felicity, when things got busy. Viv would be baby-sitting almost full-time this week.

Madame Pong did not pay her staff as much as they felt they deserved, but there had been other compensations. Whenever Adelaide felt resentful, she reminded herself of this fact. Sometimes, it was harder to persuade Viv. Viv felt that Madame Pong was a bully.

The number of crates exported each year was evidence of their success. Adelaide checked the latest numbers. One hundred and twenty crates, each containing fifty Squidgy Dinosaurs, would be delivered to the *Yen-Ting* over the next week. Six thousand dinosaurs – their largest shipment yet – would soon be making their way to Taiwan with the departing guests. She closed the file and took a dainty sip of her Nescafé, now lukewarm. Bruce would start moving the dinosaurs today. Everything was jingle-bang on schedule. Adelaide was pleased. No, Madame Pong had nothing to worry about.

Then, at 8 a.m. on the dot, the phone rang and threw Adelaide's ordered world upside down.

'Adelaide? Pong here. I need one thousand more dinosaurs on the next shipment. That is correct. One thousand. I've already hired the gougers. The extra films for Movie Man will be on the *Yen-Ting*.'

Outside Adelaide's office, the sprinklers went *tkkk, tkkk, tkkk* – oblivious to Adelaide's distress. She stood up and checked the time. 8.20 a.m. Her mind was whirring round as well. *An extra thousand dinosaurs!* Bruce and Viv were going to be furious! Adelaide was too flustered to be angry. She simply did not know if she could do what Madame Pong had ordered.

Dodging the sprinklers, she ran across the lawn to her modest brick bungalow, to break the news to her husband. Bruce would have to travel ASAP to Gun Carriage Island and inform Movie Man that they needed another two thousand crystals.

She raced up the stairs and stood panting at Felicity's bedroom door. She was still asleep, thank goodness. But the door of the *en-suite* bathroom was locked. Bruce was having his morning soak. The radio was blaring news of the weather conditions at Lords in England, where the Ashes were being played. The water was running. She knocked, but he couldn't hear. Knowing that it could be another hour – like his cricket, Bruce took these energizing soaks very seriously – Adelaide slowly descended the stairs. She would let him enjoy his last hour of peace and then break the news. He'd been *so* looking forward to the Ashes.

She returned to her office, too preoccupied to worry about the wet grass marks on her vintage buckskin shoes. She picked up the phone and dialled Viv's number.

Chapter 7

'Viv, it's me. Adelaide. I'm not waking you am I?'

'Are you kidding? Those wretched peacocks got me up at five!'

Adelaide cut right to it. 'Madame Pong wants an extra thousand dinosaurs.'

'*What*? When?'

'On the return boat with the guests.'

'Are you joking? How are we going to make a thousand dinosaurs in seven days?'

'I know. But she's already hired the gougers.'

Viv was silent.

'Are you still there?'

'That's bad,' said Viv at last. 'That really stinks. It's *awful* news.'

'We don't have a choice,' said Adelaide.

Viv laughed, incredulously. 'Well maybe *you* don't have a choice, love, but I reckon *I do*. I reckon I'm the one in the 'quation with the least amount of money and the most amount of choice, now that I come to think about it.'

'What do you mean?' asked Adelaide nervously.

'First, there are no feathers. You get me? *No feathers*. Unless you want to send her a lot of beige dinosaurs?'

'That's not an option,' said Adelaide tartly.

'Second, I have a store to run, remember? I'm a busy person even without all this Eekobeasties business.'

'Would a bonus help?'

Viv's tone softened immediately. 'How much?'

'Five hundred.'

'That's not very generous.'

'OK, make it a thousand.'

'Now you're talking! Maybe I'll find some loose feathers in the hay.'

'Surely, there's ways to make them go further? During the war, my mother made one cabbage last a week.'

'Well we're not at war, are we!' said Viv crisply. 'No, what I really need is one fresh, feathered bird. Can't you get Madame Pong to find one in Taipei and express-post it?'

'You clearly know nothing about customs or quarantine, Viv.'

'Anyway, there's another problem. Supposing I get hold of a peacock – which is veryhighlyunlikely – and say we tried to make an extra thousand dinosaurs – what are you going to do 'bout Felicity?'

'Felicity?'

'I can't baby-sit Felicity *and* make a thousand extra dinosaurs *and* run my store,' she huffed. 'I'm not *Superwoman*, you know.'

'I'll find someone else to help with Felicity.'

'I'll tell you what you ought to do with that ankle-biter! Dump her naughty little bottom on a chair in school, where it belongs.'

'Don't start this,' said Adelaide, tight-lipped. 'You know she won't go.'

'Don't give her a choice, then.'

Adelaide was furious. How dare Viv try to tell her how to bring up her child! The time was ticking on.

'Or get your husband to take care of her.'

'He has to get the—'

'Get the what? *What?*'

'Nothing,' said Adelaide quickly. 'Anyway, *Bruce does not do children*.'

'Strewth! What's wrong with the bloke?' raved Viv. 'With all due respect, Adelaide, sometimes you act like a 1950s housewife! This is the modern era! Yoo hoo! Wakey wakey! Even Aussie men have been known to take care of their own kids these days.'

'Forget about Felicity,' said Adelaide icily. 'I'll deal with my daughter. You deal with the feathers.'

Chapter 8

For two days the *Loki* remained trapped in the white-out.

After the initial shock of their predicament had subsided, the family ran out of things to say about it. They tried to carry on as before, but Thora kept feeling unnaturally sleepy, as if her entire body were filling with sand.

The whole situation was too 'sir real', as she put it. Her heart went out to Mr Walters. She could see the anxiety in the corners of his mouth as he wiped the fog from his photo of Imogen in Battery Point.

To be so close to Hobart and yet so distant!

Almost as bad, he couldn't listen to the Ashes.

So they waited and they watched, like the hosts of a party hoping that the great white unwanted guest would just pack up and leave and let them get on with it.

Though the boat did not appear to be moving, they were not entirely sure. They had no reference points to go by. And without clues, they occasionally imagined the worst. Especially Mr Walters, who had taken to napping in a director's chair on deck.

He was sound asleep when Thora came up beside him with her journal in her hand and noticed that something had changed.

Her ponytail was streaming south like telltales on a yacht. The water ahead had darkened with small ripples. She poked Mr Walters' shoulder. 'Mr Walters, wake up! We're moving! Really and truly!'

'Ouch!' said Mr Walters, opening one eye.

Mr Walters had grown so thin and frail this past year that the gentlest prod could bruise him. 'I don't know what's come over me. I just can't fight these little naps!'

'The fog is thinning,' cried Halla joyfully. 'Look! A patch of blue!'

'Nine o'clock,' said Mr Walters, checking his watch. 'We've been in that wretched cloud for forty-eight hours to the dot.'

The group watched the mist melt away, revealing a cobalt sky, a choppy blue-grey sea and once again, a view of the coast.

'What have we here?' asked Mr Walters, frowning.

'Hobart!' exclaimed Thora.

'I don't think so.'

Thora grabbed the binoculars and examined the rugged boulders that lined the stretch of coast on their starboard side. 'It doesn't exactly look like a big-city port,' she conceded.

'And there's a good reason why not. That could only be Flinders Island!' said Mr Walters, studying the chart. 'We've travelled hundreds of kilometres due north! Past Oyster Bay, Wineglass Bay, Bennalong and St Helen's. *How is this possible?*' His face bore a strange expression.

But Thora wasn't really listening. 'Flinders! Hey, Cosmo! Come here and get your first glimpse of home! We're going to find your family!'

Then she remembered Mr Walters' plans. 'I *am* sorry. You wanted to visit Hobart first. Well, let's turn back!'

'Easier said than done, Thora. The engine's still out. And we're travelling in the opposite direction.

It's two and a half days back to Hobart – and that's being optimistic!'

Mr Walters was straining to steer the boat. The wind was not blowing hard, yet the *Loki* was resisting all his efforts. They were moving exceptionally fast. 'Give me a hand, would you Thora? Here, grab the wheel.'

'The *Loki* seems to have a mind of her own,' observed Halla nervously.

'Maybe we're caught in some sort of current,' sang Thora, scanning the sea. She was so elated to see the sky and waves that she had not fully grasped the danger of their situation.

'Turn her to starboard!' said Mr Walters. 'We'll anchor at Flinders.'

But even working together, Thora and Mr Walters could not correct the *Loki*'s course. The boat continued to gather speed, paying no heed to their desire to land.

'We've got to stop her,' said Mr Walters. 'We're not prepared for what's ahead.'

Though he spoke calmly, Thora heard the razor edge to his words. 'Ahead' was Bass Strait, which was famous for huge, wild storm-waves. Winds of seventy-eight knots. It had wrecked hundreds of ships, some of which had disappeared without trace.

The wind was picking up, too. And the swells were growing in size.

'A rock!' shouted Mr Walters.

Another thing that made the strait so lethal was the large number of half-submerged reefs. The one ahead rose out of the water like a huge grey elephant back. Thora held her breath. Clasping the projectionist's ring for luck, she locked eyes with Halla.

There was a sharp scraping sound of wood brushing something harder. The boat shivered as if it had struck its funny bone. Then stopped. Mr Walters' radio flew off the table and landed with a bump at Thora's feet, knocking the aerial out of its pivot joint. The *Loki* tilted sideways.

Thora scooped up the radio seconds before a wave washed the deck.

'Hang on!' Mr Walters hollered.

Another wave slammed into the *Loki*'s side just as a loud whistle caught their attention.

Not twenty metres away stood a man in a crayfish boat. He was waving a rope.

'Prepare to receive!' cried Thora.

The man pulled up alongside and with quick, expert hands attached the rope to the railing and threw his boat into reverse.

The *Loki* righted.

The family gasped with relief. By some miracle, they had avoided capsizing.

The *Loki* groaned – as if it knew the game was over – and at that moment, the engine sputtered to life. Mr Walters untied the rope and the crayfish boat sped ahead of them.

Less than an hour later, the *Loki* muddled its way into a harbour on Flinders' south-west coast. The man in the rescue boat directed them to the only vacant berth, beside a colossal, pink luxury ocean liner called the *Yen-Ting*.

The smell of diesel fuel hit them powerfully.

'Not what I would have expected,' Mr Walters said quietly.

After tying up, Mr Walters and Thora went to thank their mysterious red-haired rescuer.

'No worries,' he replied. 'There are people in Blackie's Bother who can service your engine.'

'Blackie's Bother?' queried Thora.

But he had jogged down the jetty and out of sight.

'A true-blue Aussie bloke,' said Mr Walters appreciatively.

In ten years of travelling the oceans, this had been their most hair-raising landing by far.

to hangars
old airport
RAZOR wir
fence
Wheely's
BLACKIE'S BOTHER
Petrol station
Post
Main Street
Parking
orange lichen
cray fishing b
Loki
JETTY
Yen

nctuary ↗

elicity's house

Treatment rooms

Pool

Aqua Solarium

DEEP BREATH HOTEL

Hardware Store

Barbies

Farm

Sheep

wallabies

echidna

BIG BOULDERS

TIGER SNAKE

more boulders

KANGAROO BAY

To GUN Carriage Island

Chapter 9

For a few minutes, nobody said another word.

The family were no strangers to odd events. Halla was a mermaid after all. But they had never before lost control of the *Loki*.

Mr Walters looked down at his trembling hands. The cliché *swept out to sea* had taken on fresh significance. He popped a Polo Mint into his mouth, too rattled to offer them around.

They had come *so* close.

Halla reached over and took Mr Walters' shaking hand into her own. 'Maybe this detour was meant to be. As Thora said, in Australia everything is topsy-turvy. It makes sense to start back to front.'

'I'm not sure I'm up to living the day in reverse,' said Mr Walters, referring to the Hysteron-Proteron Club from his university days.

'It can be quite fun to eat dinner for breakfast,' offered Thora, 'but walking backwards all day is downright dangerous!'

'Anyway,' said Halla, 'we can visit Flinders and move on to Hobart later.'

'And you, Cosmo, can meet your family!' said Thora, turning a cartwheel on the deck.

Cosmo hopped out of her way.

Halla made no more mention of the strange, almost irresistible magnetic pull out to sea. Nor had the feeling entirely left her, but she hardened herself against it. The most important people in her life stood before her now.

'Tea?' suggested Thora.

'Smashing idea,' said Mr Walters with a weak smile.

Thora returned a few minutes later, carrying a pewter tray that held a pot of tea, cups and saucers, milk and sugar, teaspoons and the last packet of Jaffa Cakes left

from their stay in England. It was the family's custom to celebrate big events with a piping hot pot of Russian Caravan.

'There's not much in life that isn't improved by a good cup of tea,' observed Mr Walters, deliberately turning his back on the hull that soared above them in the next berth. He raised his cup. 'To our rescuer, the true-blue Aussie bloke,' he toasted.

'To Cosmo!' said Thora.

'To Flinders Island!' said Halla.

They bumped cups.

Chapter 10

Thora dropped three spoonfuls of brown sugar into her cup, and as she stirred, she glanced around the harbour. It was not exactly bustling, but there was a fair amount going on. To her left, she could see three medium-sized yachts, a number of cargo vessels, fishing boats piled high with crayfish cages, and a pair of sea kayaks. To her right, the massive cruise ship.

Her eyes ran over the bright pink stern. Unlike the peeling hull of the battered *Loki,* the ship she now studied was in mint condition. Sparkly black letters spelled out the name *Yen-Ting*. The height and girth of the vessel and the way it sat so confidently in its berth reminded Thora of the great female sumo wrestler Phat Chance, whom she had seen perform once in Tokyo after Halla swam the Tama River. Thora had marvelled at the girl's tiny head and small ears with their delicate garnet earrings. She remembered the wrestler's hands and feet with their pink-painted nails, and how funny they looked at the end of her huge pillowy arms and

legs. Despite the feminine details, Phat Chance could squash whatever lay in her path into a Japanese omelette. The *Yen-Ting* looked like it could, too.

'Pity,' said Mr Walters, without turning around. 'I was almost certain that Flinders would be free of such vulgarity.'

'I was hoping for something a little more remote too,' admitted Halla, scanning the fishing boats. 'Maybe we could move on until we find somewhere more private?'

'According to the guidebook, there are plenty of small bays around the island,' said Mr Walters. 'But the *Loki* needs an overhaul, and as our rescuer advised, Blackie's Bother is the place. Besides, this will be a good spot to catch a radio signal.'

'That's right!' said Thora. 'The Ashes in England! But you'll have to listen to it at a topsy-turvoid time.'

'From 7 p.m. to 3 a.m., not bad. Missing sleep is a small sacrifice for the great game,' said Mr Walters solemnly.

Mr Walters had taught Thora to play 'the great game' when she was knee-high to a set of stumps. And he always encouraged her to follow the 'Tests' on the radio. But the truth was, Thora never really had understood the point of them. They were harder than any calculus or geometry tests that Mr Walters sometimes set her.

'I'd forgotten,' said Halla. Thora's mother did not even *pretend* to understand cricket. It had never been played on the ocean floor. 'I can always explore a little on my own. But, Thora, it looks as though we will need your legs—'

'At your service!' exclaimed Thora. 'Are we low on supplies?'

Halla calculated. 'All we've got left is a tub of Gentleman's Relish, half an angel food cake, and some freeze-dried shrimp brine.'

The shrimp brine had belonged to Shirley. How Thora missed the 'little Empress', as Mr Walters had called her.

'Get your feathers in order, Cosmo,' Thora shouted. 'We're about to feel the land of your rellies under our feet!'

Thora polished off the last Jaffa Cake and dashed into her room to pull out the old tea chest she kept under her bed. It contained all of her treasures, including some money left over from the family's visit to Sydney when Thora was six. She counted out thirty dollars and forty-five cents. 'Oops,' she exclaimed, picking out a Canadian quarter, three American dimes and a British five-pound note. 'Foreign currents won't buy much tucker!'

Outside, Mr Walters was seated beside his radio, digging around in his tool box. 'I'm going to straighten the aerial and then tie the radio to the mast. I have a feeling that if I mount it high enough, I'll catch the signal for the broadcast.'

'Of course!' said Thora.

Cosmo fluffed his feathers at his reflection in the window and joined her. His excitement reminded Thora of the first time she had visited her father's home town, Grimli-By-The-Sea. She remembered how she felt when her eyes first saw what her father's eyes had seen; when her feet first walked the roads he had once travelled too. Now it was Cosmo's turn.

'Let's go.'

'Mind yourself, Thora,' Halla shouted.

Chapter 11

The sun beat down as Thora and Cosmo climbed off the boat and walked along the wooden jetty.

On the beach, Thora turned to survey the harbour. The turquoise water was the exact colour of the Windex that Mrs Grubb used to spray-clean her windows back in Grimli. Bordering the bay, a snow-white ribbon of sand ran as far as the eye could see. It was low tide, and countless shallow pools had formed in the winking sand. A number of boats bobbed on the edge of the

water. And further down the beach Thora saw clam pickers, a few young children climbing rocks and a scruffy dog chasing oyster catchers and barking joyfully. After such a long sea voyage and strange landing, it was good to feel the ground again between her toes. Cosmo spread his tail feathers and scratched the sand with his claw. He seemed to feel the same way.

A few paces along, they paused to watch a diver strapping on his equipment: snorkels, flippers, weights. When he turned and removed his sunglasses, Thora jumped back. Their rescuer! 'The true-blue Aussie bloke!'

He looked different in his yellow wetsuit and electric-blue diving jacket with a hood from which a wisp of red hair poked out. She leaned over to shake his hand vigorously.

'You really saved our bacon back there.'

Thora peered towards his boat, which was anchored to a buoy off-shore – the same boat that had rescued the *Loki*. 'Are you going to look for shipwrecks? Mr Walters says Bass Strait is stuffed with them.'

'Abalone,' said the man. His eyes widened as he noticed Cosmo.

'No, it's true!' said Thora indignantly. 'Not baloney at all.'

The man squeezed his fingers into a pair of tight gloves. 'Abalonesafish,' he replied.

'Pardon me?'

'Afish!'

'Funny, I always thought baloney was a meat – the chewy pink stuff with lard polka dots. I had *no idea* that divers caught baloney in the sea. That's what I love about arriving in a new place: you learn so many interesting new facts of life.'

'You got the chewy bit right. Abalonesaschewy as a Squidgy Dinosaur.'

Thora took a moment to let his words sink in. Australians certainly spoke fast, their words piling up and running together like the dodgem cars she had ridden at the Barford St John summer fete.

'I've never tried dinosaur meat,' she responded. 'I always thought they were extinguished.'

'Move out of the way, little nipper,' said the man, as he started to wade to his boat.

'No worries,' said Thora, trying out an Australian phrase she'd heard some yachties use off the New Zealand coast.

The man rinsed his goggles in the sea-water. 'How long you folks here?' he asked.

Thora shook her head. 'Not sure.'

'Blow-ins,' he mumbled, nodding his head.

'Blow-ins?'

'Blow in, blow out. Like the wind.'

'Maybe ...' she said.

His tone told her 'blow-in' was not a compliment. But you never really knew with Aussies. Mr Walters said they liked to take the mickey out of a Pom – which, translated, meant they liked to tease people from Britain (like Mr Walters). 'It's when they're polite that you have to worry,' he'd warned Thora.

'Just don't take that bird with you round town,' the man warned as he put on his goggles. 'People 'round here can be funny 'bout peacocks.' And with that he dived underwater.

Thora was pleased to have made contact with their rescuer: her first real Australian baloney diver. And she was chuffed that he'd been a little bit rude to her.

Even so, his final warning rang in her ears. It didn't really surprise her, for she had met many people over the years who didn't like peacocks. (Peacocks were, after all, exceedingly vain, often rude and sometimes very loud!) But it was disappointing for Cosmo, who was ripe and ready to be reunited with his family.

She led a sullen Cosmo back to the *Loki*, instructing him to remain within sight of the boat. 'There's still a lot to explore around the harbour,' she consoled him. 'I'll get the groceries and ask some questions in town.'

'No point in upsetting the locals,' added Mr Walters, ruffling Cosmo's feathers affectionately. Thora had filled him in on her conversation with the baloney diver.

Cosmo looked like he was about to peck Mr Walters' hand.

Thora headed up the hill, her footsteps sending up plumes of dust. The landscape around her was dry. Everything in sight was silvery-brown, the shade of wombat fur, even the road leading into town. The scrub on either side was a scramble of twigs, dead branches and dust. 'Perfect if you're an undercover snake,' she said, 'but not so good if you're an undercover mermaid.' Mr Walters' warning about Australia's deadly snakes came back to her, and she stomped one of her windsurfing slippers to scare off whatever might be lurking in the undergrowth. Halla had read that the snakes were even more plentiful on the smaller islands around Flinders, especially Gun Carriage.

The houses that lined the road into Blackie's Bother were surprisingly small. 'Like cookie-cutter doll houses,' observed Thora. 'Not a lot of room inside to do cartwheels or practise the highland fling.'

She continued into town, passing a gift shop with swimming costumes, T-shirts and toy dinosaurs in the window; a chemist with a window display of summer hats and sun lotion; a hardware store ('I do love inner decorating,' Thora said with a sigh. 'I wonder if they sell plastic flamingos'). When she came to the Blackie's Bother Bakery, she went in and bought a half-dozen cream doughnuts. Cosmo's favourite.

Chapter 12

Finally, at the end of the main street, Thora spotted Wheely's Grocery Shop. The name was written in large black letters and underneath it in red: WE WILL NOT DISAPPOINT. The notice board beside the entrance contained a number of handwritten messages:

Charity Swim to Gun Carriage ISLAND. Hosted by the FLINDERS MEDICAL CENTRE. SPONSOR SHEETS AVAILABLE WITHIN. Don't forget the banquet! free for ALL PARTICIPANTS.

CHOOK POO – Free if you come and collect it.
* ~~See~~ Gemma within
Smell

Someone had changed the word 'See' to 'Smell'.

Thora entered, grabbed a rickety shopping cart and began one of her favourite kinds of journey: a trip up the aisle of a foreign shop.

Despite the murky lighting and oaty smell, the place was a hodgepodge of thrilling odds and ends. It was a true general store, selling everything from food to toys to kitchenware and clothing. In the Local Items section, Thora saw hand-burned boomerangs, fake Aboriginal necklaces, shell soap-dishes, plastic mutton-bird eggs, bits of porcelain claimed to be from old shipwrecks, steel-toed Blundstone boots, fishing tackle, emu oil, leatherwood honey, lavender shampoo, stuffed koalas – and more toy dinosaurs, which had a shelf of their own with a sign that read:

Thora picked one up, remembering the words of the baloney diver. The dinosaur sported two small marble eyes and had an interesting phosphorescence, not entirely foreign to Thora's half-mermaid eyes. But the spongy material felt rather damp to touch, as if it was made of wet kid leather. She placed it back on the shelf with a shudder. She had never much cared for dinosaurs. She far preferred her animals alive.

She headed over to the food aisles. Over the years, she had discovered that every country smelled different, and every country had its own weird and wonderful foods. Travelling had made Thora an adventurous eater. She had sampled simmered brains in Paris. Pig feet in Frankfurt. Seal flipper pie in St John's, Newfoundland. She had gobbled tripe and crunched on locusts. Mr Walters had taught her to have an open mind when it came to food, and she'd try almost anything.

But not Gentleman's Relish, Mr Walters' favourite anchovy spread. He'd told her that it was an acquired taste – which basically meant that she might like it when she was very old.

She pushed the cart over towards the biscuit section. It took up three whole shelves! She limited herself to five different kinds: Tim Tams, Mint Slices, Monte Carlos, Chocolate Butternut Snaps and Iced VoVos. From the cake shelf she picked out a large box of lamingtons. 'On to the savouries,' she said, pushing her cart past a sign:

She stopped to scan the collection of old kettles, chipped mugs, puzzles in smashed boxes, children's clothes. She wondered about the meaning of 'pre-loved'. Loved by its owner, but not loved enough to keep?

Did that make Shirley pre-loved as she headed out on her own into the big seas? Had Thora's own father 'pre-loved' her? Probably not: he had never known her!

A big bald man and his daughter suddenly thundered up the aisle. They were arguing about an object that the girl had snatched from the Pre-Loved shelf.

Thora stepped closer to see what it was: a megaphone! Exactly like the one that Mr Walters had used from the deck of the *Loki* to shout encouragement to Halla while she swam.

'Put it back!' said the man. 'You make enough noise as it is!'

'No!' cried the girl. 'I need it!'

The man's pointed ears gave him the air of a leprechaun, but there was nothing sprightly about the way his sturdy body filled the aisle. The girl looked about five or six; she was wiry, with a filthy face and bare feet. She wore a hessian sack pulled over her body, and her skinny brown arms bore an impressive number of purple scabs and scrapes. A braid hung down her back like a frayed rope and dangling from a grotty red ribbon were three seagull feathers.

Her father made a move to grab the megaphone.

The girl walked backwards, straight into Thora.

'Ouch! That's my foot you're smushing!' said Thora.

'You oughta git outa *my* way,' retorted the girl,

spinning around. 'I don' have eyes in the back of my head, you know!' She crossed her arms and marched huffily back to her father.

Thora shook her head and looked for the condiments.

Gentleman's Relish was almost impossible to find outside of Great Britain, so she'd have to buy something else to tempt Mr Walters. She selected a jar of pickled brown onions, some Fountain sweet chilli sauce and a six-pack of Bundaberg ginger beer.

At the back of the store her mouth watered. A sign read:

Freshest Meat Pies in town!

Thora knocked on the counter and yelled out 'Yoo-hoo', and presently a woman appeared, wiping her hands on a grimy apron. She was short and square, with blackcurrant hair and a brown leathery face. Her nose was shaped like a potato. A little tag on her shirt said VIV.

'WhatcanIdoforyou?' she asked.

'Pardon?' said Thora. 'Are you Gemma Within? If so, I do not want any chook poo. And I certainly don't want to smell you.'

'Can-I-help-you?'

'I'd like some meat pies and sausages,' said Thora. 'Pork chipolatas.'

'Only sell beef snags here. Perfect for the barbie. Howmanyyouwant?'

'What's a snag? What's a barbie?' asked Thora. The only Barbie she knew belonged to her friend Holly de Mare; *that* Barbie was a doll with blonde nylon hair, long bendy legs and a boyfriend named Ken.

'A snag is a sausage. A barbie is a barbecue. I asked you how many.'

'Two dozen of each, please,' said Thora.

'You're a tourist.'

It was more an accusation than a question.

'Never,' said Thora. 'A *traveller*.'

'What's the accent?'

'I don't believe I have an accent,' said Thora.

'Well, to my ears you soun' like an American. Or a little Pom. An, anyway, shouldn' you be in school?'

Thora had slalomed her way through these sorts of conversations a hundred times before and had learned that it was best to stop them in their tracks – before word got around and school officials started snooping.

'I'm home-schooled by my Guardian Angle, who's a very esoterical man of the world. I'm up to date in all my subjects. So no worries.'

'Not another one!' Viv scoffed. 'Home-schooling is for the birds. Ankle-biters oughta to be in school at this time of day.' She wrapped two dozen beef pies and sausages in red and white checked paper and slapped the parcel into Thora's outstretched hands.

'Thanks!' said Thora, again rather pleased at the woman's familiar rudeness. 'Oh, and Viv? Would you know where on Flinders I'd begin an epical search for the long-lost relatives of my pet peacock?'

Viv fixed her with a dark look. 'Your pet *what?*'

'Peacock.'

'Is this some sort of gag?'

'I'm sorry?'

'You have a *peacock?*'

'Yes. He was a gift to my mother many years ago. He's an Indian Blue, born right here on Flinders. We're hoping to link him up with his relatives. We're not sure exactly what he'll feel when he sees them. But we feel he has to meet them. It's sort of an ineventuality. Then he can make up his own mind about whether to stay with us or not.'

'Where is your peacock now?' asked Viv, a new note in her voice.

'Cosmo's on the boat. Or on a rock nearby! The true-blue Aussie with the red hair, who rescued us this morning in his crayfishing boat, told me—'

'Red hair? Fishing boat? That'll be my nephew,' interrupted Viv, the wrinkles on her forehead gathering together in an accordion pleat.

'Really? That's island life for you! Everybody knows everybody. Well, *he* said not to bring my peacock round town because they're not very popular – which is sad, but understandable.'

'Well, waddya know!' said Viv, shaking her head. 'Is the bird in good nick?' she asked hopefully.

'Oh yes! His feathers are spectaculatory!'

'Is that so!'

'Yes, ma'am! Do you have any ideas about where we might start our search?'

Viv was now staring at her with rapt attention.

'We'd like him to have a reunion with his rellies,' continued Thora. 'Maybe even an Aussie barbecule!'

'Perfect!' exclaimed Viv, oblivious to the customers growing impatient behind Thora. 'I mean – how long are you staying?'

Thora shrugged. 'As long as it takes to fix our boat and listen to the Ashes ...'

'Beauty!'

'Viv,' said the woman behind Thora, 'I'm in a rush here.'

Thora bowed and stepped aside. 'I'll see you round,' she said, wheeling her cart over to the checkout. What a nice woman Viv is, she thought. It makes all the difference when people are interested and ask questions!

As Thora began to unload her supplies at the checkout, the dirty-faced urchin cut the queue and shoved the megaphone into the checkout girl's hands. 'Beat ya!' she said to Thora with a neat jab of an elbow. 'Put it on the account, Gemma, will ya?'

Before running off, the girl pointed the megaphone at Thora and made a loud flatulent noise: *phhhhleeeeeegggh*! 'See you in Hobart, ya big fat fart!'

Gemma was apologetic. She rang Thora's order through and handed her the change. 'Wanna sponsor me?' she asked. 'I'm entering the Charity Swim. Every cent helps.'

'Sure,' said Thora, giving her fifty cents. She would like to have asked Gemma more – about the feral little girl and the Charity Swim – but it was time to get back to the *Loki*. 'Good luck with it!'

Thora left Wheely's carrying seven bags of supplies, including a jumbo Violet Crumble bar. She loved the gold and royal-purple wrapper. She remembered the large box of Violet Crumbles that Halla had been given when she won Cosmo in Melbourne. But after a month at sea, the honeycomb had turned wet and mushy, the chocolate to liquid. They'd been forced to throw the whole lot out in the end.

'A trickster of a girl – but that Viv lady was fair-dinkum,' said Thora, striding along.

chapter 13

'Adelaide? It's Viv.'

'I can't speak. I'm sorting out schedules. These guests are proving particularly demanding. They change their minds every five minutes.'

'How's Bruce coping?' Viv asked, unable to suppress a snicker.

'He's finding it difficult. He's not used to taking care of Felicity.'

'You can thank me, then. *He* can thank me, too!'

'For what?'

'I've solved all your problems!'

'Is that so?'

'I've found another peacock – and a baby-sitter into the bargain.'

chapter 14

Cosmo honked urgently from his perch on the roof of the *Loki* when he saw Thora return.

Thora rushed on board and dumped everything on the deck. 'Cosmo! Is everything all right?'

Cosmo shook his head and gestured with his beak.

'Over here!' came Halla's anxious voice.

Thora ran around to the other side of the cabin. 'What is it?' she called anxiously.

'I don't know what to do!' cried Halla.

Mr Walters was standing on a chair on the deck. In one hand he held the radio aerial. In the other, a pair of pliers. He was pale and his hair flopped awkwardly over his face.

'Mr Walters, what's happened?' Thora had never seen his face so white, so forlorn. 'Why are you just *standing* there?'

'I'm going to miss a cracking game!'

Halla cut in. 'He was trying to hang the radio on the mast.'

'The Ashes,' responded Thora.

'I'm afraid I gave myself a little shock.'

Thora jumped back, causing Mr Walters to sway.

'A *shock*? Did you burn yourself? Oh, dreary me!'

'Not an *electrical* shock, dear girl!'

'He's put his back out,' explained Halla.

'Yes, I shocked myself when I twisted the wrong way. There was a burning feeling and then my back seized up. I can't seem to, well, bend properly. The pain is quite extraordinary!' Though his lips moved, the rest of him was stiff.

Thora helped him down. He leaned heavily on her shoulder as they made their way slowly back to the cabin. But at least he was walking. Well, shuffling.

'You must lie down,' she ordered. 'If you can. Can you?'

'I'm not so sure,' said Mr Walters, grimacing.

'Then be very still! As still as the *Loki* in the doldrums. I'm going to, um – how about a cup of tea?' she asked, anxiously.

'Tea? Yes, OK.' When Thora had left, Mr Walters stared up the ceiling, which was only centimetres from his face. 'I am a foolish old man,' he murmured.

In the kitchen, Thora turned on the kettle. Whatever had happened to her Guardian Angle was probably more serious than he was letting on.

Just then, through the window, a flash of red caught her eye. It was their Aussie rescuer, chatting with the captain of the *Yin-Tang*. Just the man! Thora ran outside and called to him.

'Mr Boloney Diver! Could you lend us a hand here? We've got another problem!'

Chapter 15

His name was Trevor.

He didn't know much about First Aid, but he knew somebody who might help them. 'Her name is Adelaide and she runs The Deep Breath Hotel with her husband, Bruce.'

'Deep Breath Hotel?' asked Thora. 'What's that?'

Trevor explained that the hotel perched on the cliffs overlooking the southern part of Kangaroo Bay, where

the passengers from the *Yen-Ting* were staying, was a luxury spa with healing baths.

'But does Adelaide know about injuries?' asked Thora doubtfully. 'We don't need a whirly-spa, we need a doctor! Someone who knows about muscles, tenderloins and liggy-mints!'

'The doctor's away. She works off the island on Tuesdays and Wednesdays,' shrugged Trevor. 'But if you want to go to the hotel, I can give you a lift over in my Combi.'

Thora realised that the options were limited. 'It's worth a try,' she said, leading Trevor into the *Loki*.

Chapter 16

Halla had disappeared when she heard Trevor's voice, but not before covering the pizza-sized hole on the living-room floor with a heavy Persian carpet.

Cosmo sat on it with a mournful expression on his face.

'Does that bird live in the boat with you?'

'Yes,' said Thora.

'You know, I meant what I said. Keep him out of sight.'

'But he *lives* here,' said Thora. 'I can't put him under cabin arrest. It wouldn't be right.'

She knocked on Mr Walters' door and introduced Trevor. 'He's a baloney diver, aren't you, Trevor?'

'Abalone,' said Trevor.

'Abalone?' murmured Mr Walters. His tone was reverential. 'I last ate abalone on my honeymoon. What a luxury that was.'

Mr Walters' face had gone from white to a sort of grey colour. His lips stuck together when he tried to speak. But he managed to seat himself on the edge of the bed and to loosen the collar of his shirt. He fished in his pocket for another Polo Mint.

Thora passed him a glass of water. 'Have a sip,' she ordered.

Trevor told Mr Walters about The Deep Breath Hotel, and to Thora's surprise, Mr Walters was willing to go there if Trevor was willing to drive him. 'I don't know how to thank you.'

'No worries,' said Trevor.

Insisting that he use them as human crutches, Mr Walters allowed Thora and Trevor to navigate him into Trevor's Combi at the dockside parking lot. Five minutes later, they pulled into the wide driveway of The Deep Breath Hotel & Spa.

Chapter 17

The tall white fence and iron gate reminded Thora of the condo-complexes she'd seen near the John Wayne Airport in Orange County, California. And the method of entry was the same. Trevor had to speak with someone at the end of an intercom, who in turn buzzed them in. 'It's fairly high security,' he explained.

'Why?'

'That's the way rich people like it.'

Thora whistled as the hotel came into view.

The hotel resembled an enormous white marshmallow that had been heated and stretched in many directions.

There was no overhanging roof, no main door, and only two windows, which were large and round and seemed to track them as they drove past.

The grass surrounding the hotel was a shade of bright green that made Thora think of Shirley.

'The rooms are all white on the outside, but the interiors are wild. Stripes, swirls, lava lamps – very showy.'

'You work here?' asked Thora.

'Odd jobs,' he replied. 'A family connection.'

They drove up the gently sloping road and then turned down a narrower road towards a nondescript red-brick house under the shade of three eucalypts. The house's chief feature was a big old-fashioned verandah that reminded Thora of those she'd seen on *estancias* outside Buenos Aires.

'You wait here,' Trevor said, running his fingers through his hair. He walked up the low stairs, across the deck to the door and knocked. When no one answered, he jumped down and dashed across the lawn to the white building a hundred metres away.

'Oh, dear. He's going to a lot of trouble,' said Mr Walters.

A few minutes later, Trevor returned with a Barbie

doll of a woman at his side. Her white-blonde hair was big and starchy-looking and everything she wore matched: the eyeshadow, the skirt, the clutch bag and the shoes were all roughly the same shade of baby-blue.

'Adelaide Ferguson,' said Trevor.

Thora held out her hand. 'I'm Thora Greenberg.'

'Are you the baby-sitter?' Adelaide asked.

'Don't think so,' said Thora, shaking her head. She couldn't stop staring at the woman's hair-do. 'I'd hate to squash an ankle-biter.'

'Didn't you speak to Viv?'

'That nice lady at Wheely's?' said Thora. 'Well, yes, in fact, and we covered the waterfront, but we never spoke of baby-sitting.'

Adelaide sighed. 'It must be a misunderstanding.'

'No worries – they're common as muck!' said Thora sympathetically. 'This is my Guardian Angle, Mr Walters. He's contracted an injury. Trevor said you might be able to help.'

'You've put your back out?' said Adelaide.

'It's feeling much better,' said Mr Walters.

'As Trevor probably explained, The Deep Breath is primarily an Aqua Solarium and treatment centre for our special guests. They must remain our first priority at all times.'

'Oh, yes,' said Mr Walters. 'That is perfectly understandable.'

'The hotel is full. We're flat out here.'

'Oh come on, Adelaide,' interrupted Trevor. 'They won't notice one extra person. Someone who actually *needs* help ...'

'If it's too much trouble ...' began Mr Walters.

Adelaide tossed her head. 'Well we *are* human, after all. Let me see, I have a girl here – Sha is her name. She's very good. She'll be free in a short time to give you a Reiki session.'

'Rakey?' said Thora. 'That sounds like a bad idea to me.'

'Reiki is very effective for back problems.'

'Nobody's going to *rake* Mr Walters.'

'Rake me?' said Mr Walters.

Trevor chortled.

Adelaide pressed her lips together. 'It's alternative therapy,' she said. 'It will help to realign your back. I recommend that this session be followed by a soak in the Aqua Solarium. I have a pool free at ...' She clicked open her purse and removed a white card, which she passed to Mr Walters. 'Three o'clock. We've had a cancellation.'

Mr Walters studied the card.

'There will be a fee for the service.' She pointed to the price list on the back of the card.

Mr Walters gasped.

Adelaide drummed her fingers on her purse. Her nails looked fake. 'I can offer you a ... medical discount. You look like you're in pain.'

'OK. I'll do it,' said Mr Walters, taking out his wallet.

Thora bit her tongue. He must be in *a lot* of pain.

'Very well,' said Adelaide. 'I hope it helps.'

Mr Walters counted out the bills.

'Trevor, would you mind showing your new friend the way to the treatment rooms?'

'Not at all,' said Trevor.

Before she left, Adelaide turned and looked closely at Thora. 'How old are you, by the way?'

'Almost twelve,' said Thora. 'How old are you?'

The question seemed to throw Adelaide. She patted

her hair and rushed back towards the hotel, muttering to herself.

'That's a sensitive subject,' whispered Trevor.

'It often is,' said Mr Walters, 'for women of a certain age.'

'Come on,' said Trevor. 'I'll take you to the spa.'

Trevor slowed to wait for Mr Walters. His red hair stuck out in sweaty tufts.

'Adelaide owns all this?' asked Thora.

'Not exactly,' he mumbled. 'She and her husband, Bruce, manage it. The owner lives in Asia.'

'Who actually *stays* here?' asked Thora, looking over at the individual, marshmallow-shaped guest cottages, each with their private path.

'Very rich people,' said Trevor, pointing to a building marked TREATMENT CENTRE.

The automatic glass doors opened and two plump, shiny-faced women emerged on to the deck, blinking against the sun. They wore identical white kimonos and flip-flops and both carried large bottles of water. Their combined weight made the decking shake. 'The Taipei Twins,' whispered Trevor. 'They own Madame Pong's favourite restaurant.'

'Their food must be very rich too,' observed Thora.

Trevor opened the heavy wooden door and motioned

for them to enter. 'Your Reiki will be in here.'

'Thank goodness,' said Mr Walters, leaning on the reception desk.

Thora read the sign: REMOVE YOUR SHOES.

The room inside was cool. It smelled beautiful, like the lavender fields in Provence. Low benches extended from the whitewashed wall. A glass table held a neat pile of books and a stone bust of an elephant.

'Hello, Trevor. This is Mr Walters, I presume? My name is Sha.' She had a perfectly square face with thin lips, and steel-grey deep-set eyes with circles under them. 'Adelaide called. I'm going to give you a short introductory Reiki treatment now. Then you'll have a soak in the Aqua Solarium. Follow me, please.'

'I'm off,' said Trevor. 'Take good care of the old-fella, Sha.'

'Always,' said Sha.

As she escorted Mr Walters down a corridor, she turned and called out to Thora: 'Make yourself at home in the Patience Room!'

'I'm not a patient,' said Thora.

'Hah! Good one,' said Sha. 'He'll be about an hour in total.'

Chapter 19

Thora sat in the Patience Room and opened the books: *The Art of Indian Symbols*; *The Sacroeliac Challenge*; *The Beginner's Guide to Meditation*.

'Where's *Treasure Island* when you really need it?' she asked. Absently, she performed the dust-test on the stone elephant, running her finger along his tusk. It came away with no satisfying smear of grey. 'No dirt. Can't be very healthy.'

She placed the sculpture back on the table. The elephant wobbled. 'Time to go on a colour-hunt,' she declared. 'I'd like a look at the wild rooms! This place is too like the doldrums – the air-conditioned variety!'

She was about to leave by the way she had come, when she noticed another door. She opened it and followed the corridor, with its low ceiling and paved floor, to a swing-door at the end. She pushed through into the humidity of an indoor swimming pool.

A sign read:

WELCOME to the
AQUA SOLARIUM!

PLEASE REGISTER WITH
RECEPTIONIST BEFORE
PROCEEDING

There was no receptionist, so Thora proceeded down a corridor into an over-hot courtyard with a high domed ceiling and a row of large white stone tubs emanating steam and bright lights. Classical music played softly. A dozen or so bathers reclined in the water of each tub, wearing black masks over their eyes. Their faces bore the tranquil expressions of sleeping babies. They barely stirred as Thora *smuched* past in her windsurfing slippers, waving her arms above her head like a music conductor.

One bather sat up abruptly.

'Don'tchya know it's dangerous to sleep in the bath?' Thora whispered loudly.

Suddenly her voice sounded funny in her own ears. Lights from inside the bathtubs threw off a glare that made everything swirl with tiny bright points. The tubs seemed to be moving, like so many cars in a parking lot. A few more bathers stirred. A pink-cheeked man with a goatee removed his mask and glared at her.

Thora waved at him. But something about the light was making her feel jumpy, as if she had a squirrel caught in her wetsuit. She did three cartwheels in a row and skipped over to the wooden bench by the window to wait for Mr Walters. The big floor-to-ceiling window was steamed up: with her finger, she drew a picture of Cosmo.

Suddenly a small face appeared. It was laughing, smeared with dirt, and had the same sauciness of the street kids she'd met in Bahia when Halla was swimming the Rio Da Silva.

'Now I really am seeing things!' Thora said.

It was the urchin from the 'Pre-Loved' section at Wheely's! Thora wiped off her drawing to get a better look, but the creature had vanished.

Maybe the steam and the lights were playing tricks on her.

Then a man's harsh voice echoed through the spa: 'WHERE IS SHE?'

Thora turned. The man striding toward her was very big and had lots of muscles. It was the father from Wheely's! What was *he* doing here?

'HAVE YOU SEEN FELICITY?' he barked.

'I can help you search if you like. But here in the spa I've only seen *them*,' said Thora, pointing to the bathers.

'Where'd she go, then?'

'I have no idea,' said Thora, honestly.

The man stopped and the bulge went out of his

muscles. 'Is she hiding? I left her alone – just for a few minutes. Her mother will be furious!'

'Is Felicity your daughter?'

'Yes.' The man stared at Thora as if he was seeing her for the first time. 'Who are *you*? What are *you* doin' in here? You're not with the *Yen-Ting* crowd.' He cracked his knuckles.

'I was just on my way out, now that you mention it,' said Thora. She turned and dashed for the door.

Chapter 20

Outside, the mid-afternoon heat had driven most of the people indoors, and the empty grounds buzzed with the crickety sound of the sprinkler-system.

Thora slipped behind a fat eucalyptus tree and waited. A moment later, the man emerged from the spa, looked around and headed around the back. 'Phew!' said Thora. 'The coast is clear! The sky is blue! And I'm hotter than a possum on a corrugated-tin roof!' She stepped into the spray and let the cool water drench her. Her head cleared and the funny feeling she'd had in the Aqua Solarium melted away. Overhead, some birds tussled in the trees. A few guests milled past wearing white kimonos and plastic flip-flops. In the distance she heard a splash. Wiping the water from her eyes, she noticed a large open-air swimming pool.

Closer up, she saw that the pool was rather unusual: it was shaped like a wok. One lone swimmer was doing push-ups at the edge. Otherwise, people lay sunning on the deck chairs around the pool, their arms, legs and bellies glistening with oil.

'Like snags on the Barbie!' Thora said aloud.

Some people read newspapers and sipped drinks decorated with paper umbrellas and chunks of orange-coloured fruit. A few sat on mats stretching their bodies into strange positions. A lifeguard in a long T-shirt watched over them from his perch.

Thora longed to dive in and cool herself off. But after her experience in the Aqua Solarium, she decided she would draw too much attention if she did.

But it sure was hard to walk on by!

A bell sounded over The Deep Breath intercom and people around the pool began to gather their things.

Though Thora had never attended school, she had read about how students changed classes when the bell rang. She assumed the guests were heading to their next

'class'. She watched with fascination as the grounds filled with roly-poly people in white kimonos whose accessories had the glitter of Christmas ornaments: huge sunglasses, chunky watches, thick gold rings, and for the women, handbags bigger than Mr Walters' old cricket bag, with words written on them in gold letters. Thora read a few aloud: 'Fendi, Chloe, Balenciaga.' She had seen those words at the fashion show after Halla swam Lake Dollup in Miami.

Who *were* these people?

'Excuse me, ma'am,' she said to a woman standing alone under the shade of a tree. 'Are you really and truly spending your whole vacation in Tasmania at The Deep Breath Hotel?'

The woman removed her sunglasses. 'Yes, why?'

'I was going to ask you the same question.'

'I come here every year for the Reiki and the baths.'

'Why?'

'Make me feel ten years younger,' said the woman.

'Really?' said Thora. 'Why is it that young people want to be older and old people want to be younger? I'm almost twelve, and I wouldn't want to turn the clock back and be two years old!'

'You're a rude girl,' said the woman. She replaced her sunglasses and stalked off to meet a friend.

Thora continued along the path. Windsurf slippers *shmuching*, she read the names on the marshmallow guesthouses. The letters had been burnt into boomerang-shaped signs like the ones she'd seen at Wheely's. The Supine Serpent Room; The Tickled Buddha Room; The Patient Panda Room; The Mongoose Mantra Room.

The door of The Laughing Giraffe Room suddenly opened and the dirty urchin face peeked out.

'Thisisastick-up!' The child pointed her free finger at Thora and made a click sound with her tongue. 'Hand over all yer vallybles!'

The girl had added more seagull feathers to her braid, and up close her eyes were a startling shade of light brown – almost yellow.

'You're a wanted girl,' said Thora. 'I reckon the sheriff's after you.'

'What's a sheriff?' asked the girl suspiciously.

'The head cheese,' said Thora. 'He's looking for you and he's not happy.'

'You mean my dad,' said the girl, as if Thora was a simpleton. 'Why are you all wet?'

'The sprinklers,' said Thora. 'Very refreshing! You ought to try it sometime.'

'Nah. I prefer dirt,' the girl said, reaching back into the room for a black and white football, which she then tossed up high and caught, casually, with one hand. 'I could beat you.'

'Why would you want to do that?' asked Thora.

'Whussamatter? Scared I'd win?'

'Win what?' asked Thora.

The girl scowled. 'Everything.'

Thora scratched her elbow. 'I'm not sure I understand.'

'Bet you can't ice-skate.'

Thora admitted she had never tried.

'I'm an expert at every sport – skatin', tennis, grounders, cricket, swimming—'

'Well, I might give you some competition in the water,' said Thora, turning longingly toward the pool.

'Nah, I could beat you easy. At dodge ball. Chinese checkers. Football, too.'

'OK then, let's have a game,' said Thora.

'Felicity!'

Thora looked over to see the muscly man striding towards them.

'Oh, no!' whispered Felicity. 'It's Daddy! Run!'

chapter 21

Thora chased Felicity down the path, around the treatment rooms, past the red-brick house and into the scrub behind the hotel. The girl was swift and light, even on bare feet.

'I'm the winner!' shouted Felicity, raising her arms above her head in victory.

But she had spoken too soon. Thora overtook her just as they reached the path leading up to the mountain. 'It's a draw.' Thora grinned.

'You're not even puffed!' said Felicity, admiringly. She leaned forward with the flat of her palms on her thighs and stared at the ground, panting.

'You must have tough feet,' said Thora.

'Yep. Look.' Felicity held up a dusty foot for Thora to inspect. The skin on the bottom resembled moccasin leather. 'I can't be bothered wearin' shoes,' she said. 'Too much trouble.'

'What about snakes?' said Thora. 'And spiders?'

Felicity shook her head. 'Don't bother *me*,' she said.

'They don't like my blood. An' anyway, they aren't much innerested in people less you get in their way.' She crouched down to examine a shiny black beetle, and let it crawl over the top of her hand. 'Lookit 'im. He's a sad little critter, but he could win a beauty contest fer beetles, he's so pretty!'

She reminded Thora of someone.

Felicity put the beetle down on a rock. 'Wanna see my secret place?'

'I'd be honoured,' said Thora.

'Whaddya mean?'

'Yes, please.'

'Why didn't you just say so? You use the wrong words—'

'Like what?'

'Like what you just said! And you *sound* funny, too. I never heard someone talk like you 'fore. Why do you do it?'

'There's lots of different ways of saying things,' said Thora. 'If I asked for "snags" in Snugshire, nobody would understand what I wanted.'

'A snag's a snag.'

'Some people only know it as a sausage.'

'They must be real dumb, then.'

'Not dumb,' said Thora. 'Different.'

'Whatever,' said Felicity.

Thora followed Felicity along a sandy path through the grass to a clearing in which stood a simple house constructed from black wood. The wind had blown it so that it tilted to one side.

Felicity opened the wooden door. It was a ghostly shade of bone blue, bleached by the battering of salty wind.

'Nobody lives here, don't worry,' she said, entering.

Thora followed.

The deserted room consisted of two wooden bunk beds without bedding, a three-legged table and a few basic chairs. There were a few books on the shelf. Thora was reaching for them when a huge bush rat scrambled over her hand, leaped to the floor and ran out through the partially open back door.

They followed the rat outside into a large clearing. The surrounding trees teemed with noisy birds.

'What are those?' said Thora, pointing to two enormous black shapes squabbling overhead.

'Yellow-tailed black cockatoos,' replied Felicity. There was a flash of green, too quick to follow. 'I forget what the rest are. But there's loads of every kind of bird here; you know, parrots and stuff. It used to be a sankshoo-ary.'

'You mean a sanctuary,' said Thora.

'That's what I said! But I'm not supposed to come here. Mum says there's too many snakes. Let's go!'

The girls ran back to the hotel, and along the drive to the front gate, where Mr Walters was waiting.

'I'm really the winner this time!' shouted Felicity.

'I'd call that a draw,' said Mr Walters, with the authority of an ex-umpire.

'I don't draw,' said Felicity. 'I only win! Who are you?'

'This is my Guardian Angle!' said Thora, grabbing Mr Walters' hand. 'You're standing much straighter. Did it work?'

'I believe it did,' said Mr Walters with a nod.

Thora was pleased to see him looking – and sounding – like his old self. 'Felicity, come and shake—'

'She's gone,' said Mr Walters.

Felicity was already a quarter of the way up the gravel driveway. She was belting away, without looking back, her bare feet turning up the dust.

'Good little runner,' said Mr Walters.

Chapter 22

After reviewing the dinner menu in her office, Adelaide called Viv.

'Where on earth is that baby-sitter you promised?'

'There's been a few unanticipated delays,' coughed Viv. 'I tried to talk to her today. She's staying on a houseboat in Kangaroo Bay. Unfortunately, she wasn't there.'

'Hold on a minute,' said Adelaide. 'What does this "baby-sitter" look like?'

'Funny-looking, with a ponytail and wetsuit.'

'I met her already,' said Adelaide. 'Her name is Thora Greenberg. She said she's not a baby-sitter.'

'A technicality. She will be. You'll just have to offer her a bonus.'

'She's also quite odd,' said Adelaide.

'So is Felicity!' retorted Viv. 'Anyway, we don't have time to worry about "odd".'

'And the feathers?'

'I'm almost close enough to touch them.'

Chapter 23

Trevor drove them back to the harbour parking lot and helped Mr Walters out of the Combi. 'I'm going away for a few days. I have to take some crew members from the *Yen-Ting* out fishing. I'll try and bring you some abalone.'

'That would be marvellous,' said Mr Walters.

They waved goodbye, and headed to the *Loki*.

'We must find a way to thank that man. He's been so generous with his time,' said Mr Walters.

'Australians are very commoding,' agreed Thora.

The *Loki* looked tiny next to the *Yen-Ting*, like the runt of the pod of a vast pink whale. Thora felt a wave of affection for their boat-home with its peely hull and lopsided way of sitting in the water.

Thora helped Mr Walters on board.

'Mr Walters is a partially vituperated man,' she announced to her mother as they entered the cabin.

'Thank goodness!' Halla was at the stove, peppering the soup. 'How does your back feel?' she asked.

'Remarkably better,' said Mr Walters.

'Excellent news!'

'But my stomach is remarkably empty! Something smells delicious in here!'

'Meat pies in the oven!' said Halla. 'It says on the label that they are forty per cent beef.'

'I wonder what makes up the other sixty per cent?' Thora wondered.

Halla ladled out the soup into three bowls that she garnished with dried kelp. Thora carried them to the table and then went to fetch the pies.

'Didn't you buy some ginger beer today?' Mr Walters asked Thora.

'You *must* be feeling better!' said Halla. 'Now I want to hear everything!'

As they tucked in, Mr Walters described his Reiki experience.

Halla and Thora laughed as he told them about Sha and her healing hands – hands that never even touched him. 'I have no idea how it all works,' he said. 'Or *if!*'

After the Reiki, he had been handed a sealed packet containing Lycra shorts.

'Not *Lycra,*' gasped Halla, slapping her tail. '*You?*'

The thought of Mr Walters clad in Lycra shorts made Thora giggle. 'I peeked into the Aqua Solarium and saw the bathers with their eye masks.'

Mr Walters sipped his ginger beer. 'Did you now? I didn't see you. Eye shields were mandatory in the spa bath. I was given a pair and told to meditate. So I thought about the wonderful cricket I was missing. I soaked for thirty minutes. Sha claimed that the waters were filtered by healing crystals that have the power to realign energy flows. And while naturally I do not believe in such hocus-pocus, the extraordinary thing is I feel the better for it.'

'Well, so I should hope. It cost a fortune!' said Thora.

'If you really think about it, it's rather a silly place,' Mr Walters reflected.

'Oh, come on,' said Halla. 'Little luxuries can't hurt now and then. You *never* spoil yourself.'

'In the end, I agree with Charlie Chaplin,' said Mr Walters. 'The saddest thing I can imagine is to get used to luxury.'

'I met a street kid at the hotel,' said Thora, changing the subject. 'Or at least she looks like one.'

'The runner?' asked Mr Walters.

'The Deep Breath doesn't sound like a place for children,' said Halla.

'Her name is Felicity. She's Adelaide's daughter.'

'Do you think you'll be friends?' asked Halla.

Thora shrugged. 'She's only about six years old. But you never know. She has tough feet. She can run barefoot on gravel! She's very keen on winning.'

'Nothing wrong with that,' said Mr Walters, his mind turning once more to the great game. 'In moderation.'

'It's good to keep an open mind,' said Halla.

After the dinner dishes were cleared, Thora invited Cosmo to sleep on the end of her bed. 'Don't be sad,' she said. 'We'll get started on our search soon. Mr Walters' accident today threw a bit of a short-circuit into the master plan!'

Chapter 24

Honnnnnk!

Honnnnnk!

Honnnnnk!

Thora sat bolt upright, heart thudding.

Honk!

'What *is* that crazy bird carrying on about?'

She went outside and found Cosmo perched on the *Loki*'s roof.

'Cosmo, it's five in the morning! You're going to wake up the entire southern honeysphere! Trevor told us that you mustn't draw attention to yourself.'

Honnnk!

Honnnk!

'Sushhhh!'

Honnnnk!

Cosmo pointed his beak in the direction of the water and swished his long tail feathers.

'What *is* it?'

A splash.

'Hellooo,' came a female voice.

A dark-haired woman waved from the water. She was so close that Thora could see the sprinkle of freckles on her white face.

An elusive phosphorescence in the shape of a tail. The same purple shine as Halla's.

Thora knew a mermaid when she saw one – and she also knew this one. 'Marina!' she cried.

'Thora!'

'What are you *doing*? I can't believe you're here!'

'Gosh, you sound like your mother. You two must share the same voice box! But tone it down! I'm here on the sly! Where is the old fish anyway?'

Chapter 25

'Mother!'

Thora raced in from the deck.

'Mother! It's Marina! It really is *her*!'

Halla emerged groggily from her pizza-shaped hole. 'Where?'

'Right here! I mean out there! On the stern!'

Halla slipped out and into the harbour.

The two mermaids stared at each other, shocked, delighted, half-unbelieving.

'It's really you!' cried Halla.

Marina was Halla's closest friend. The only mermaid who had not shunned Halla after she married a human and gave birth to a half-human child, Thora.

It was Marina who had held her hand when Halla sought advice from the Sea Shrew.

And it was Marina who had told Thora that Halla was in danger after Frooty de Mare captured her and displayed her in an aquarium in Grimli!

Thora watched the two happy mermaids, their grins wide as the smiles in Halloween pumpkins.

'What's going on out here?' Mr Walters emerged from his bedroom, pulling on his jumper over his shirt.

'Up early listening to the Ashes?' Thora asked.

He looked rumpled as a slept-on newspaper. 'Strange, I forgot all about it,' he said. Then he saw their guest and his eyes popped. Though he had heard about Marina, he had never met Halla's friend. He shook her hand and welcomed her.

Best-friend mermaids have the ability to track each other down no matter where they are in the world. But the swim from the Sea Floor had tired Marina.

Thora and Mr Walters helped her up through the hole in the living-room floor and urged her to rest on the sofa. To quieten her chattering teeth, Mr Walters made her a cup of sweet black tea. Halla found her a silk blanket.

'Where do I begin?' said Marina.

'My parents?' asked Halla, who had nursed a niggling worry since setting eyes on her friend. 'Has anything happened to them?'

'They're fine. They send their phosphorescence.'

'Are you sure?'

'*Yes*, I'm sure! They miss you, they really do, and they want to see you. And your sisters are fine. And so are your grandparents. But we can talk about that in a moment. I have news of a different nature.'

'Out with it,' said Halla.

Thora held her breath.

Marina's eyes shone. 'The Sea Shrew has died.'

Chapter 26

'Died,' repeated Halla.

Mr Walters started to speak. But his lips were so dry from the shock of Marina's news that he could not form the words.

Thora passed him a glass of water. 'How?' she asked.

'Natural causes,' said Marina.

Halla was quiet. She shook her head in disbelief. 'She's been there for over two hundred years ... It explains the silence of the sea.'

'Silence?' asked Marina.

'But not that strange force that carried us through Bass Strait.' Halla looked out to sea. 'The pull.'

'What are you talking about?' asked Marina.

'Later,' said Halla.

So Marina summarised the recent events.

'Last week, there was unrest on the Sea Floor. The sea horses went on strike. Students gathered in the coral reefs. Shops closed. It was rumoured that the Sea Shrew was ill and might die. Everyone began to worry who would replace her. She's been in charge of us for so long – and ruled with such an iron tail – that it was thought she would pass the crown on to her chief guard.'

A shark.

'Dreadful,' said Halla.

'Exactly the feeling everywhere. Then after two days of uncertainty, the Sea Shrew made a speech. She said she had no interest in what happened after she was gone, but nor was she going to pass on her crown. She died that afternoon.'

'Unbelievable,' said Halla.

Mr Walters clicked his false teeth.

'It *was*. When her death was announced, the ocean floor went very quiet. You could have heard a tadpole somersault. Then chaos. There was a parade. Everyone joined. They showed their colours, but they made no sound. The parade stopped at the Sea Shrew's gates. A funeral was held immediately. Nobody was sad to see her go. But already the problems have started. Serious problems.'

'What sort?' asked Mr Walters.

'The Shrew's old guard are organising. They wanted to appoint the head shark King with immediate effect. But Finnbogi has called for elections. He says it's got to be the will of the majority.'

'Who's Finnbogi?' asked Thora.

'My husband,' said Marina.

Halla stared. 'You're *married*? When? Oh Marina! What wonderful news!'

'We're coming up to our first anniversary next week,' said Marina, blushing.

'He was a student radical,' Halla told Thora. 'Nobody thought he'd ever settle down!'

'Especially me,' said Marina.

The two mermaids hugged.

Thora returned the discussion to the Sea Floor. 'All this business sounds like polly ticks,' she said, scratching her elbows, first one and then the other.

'Politics, Thora,' said Mr Walters. 'You can't escape it. Pay attention.'

'Now, that's where *you* come in, Halla,' said Marina. 'The election will be held *this* Saturday. The winners of the election will have access to the Sea Shrew's files. There may be information about Thor.'

Halla nodded.

Thora held the projectionist's ring tightly.

'I know this is all very sudden and it must sound ridiculous. *But I beg you to come back with me and vote.* Your parents sent me to tell you that *every vote matters.* Will you come, Halla?'

Halla looked over at Thora.

Thora ignored the part of her that wanted to grab her mother and beg her not to leave. 'You must go,' she said.

'Thank you, Thora,' said Halla. 'Yes, Marina, I'll come.' If there was something to find out about Thor, Halla was prepared to swim anywhere, even back to the bottom of the ocean.

Chapter 27

There was no time for a farewell party, but Mr Walters insisted that Halla eat. She would need her energy for the long swim to the Sea Floor. Marina enjoyed an extra piece of toast coated in fine-cut marmalade. She had never tasted human food and to the family's consternation their feast gave her indigestion. The strands from the marmalade were stuck in her teeth. 'Like weeds,' she said.

While Marina slept, Mr Walters washed up and Halla took a quick goodbye swim with Thora. It was still early and the few fishermen about were too absorbed in their own business to notice a mermaid and her daughter.

Halla spoke with Thora about the journey ahead. Whatever the outcome of the elections, Halla would be able to see her family. She had longed for a new start with her parents.

'They haven't forgotten you,' said Thora, snatching a farewell sniff of her mother's hair, which always smelled to her like pumpkin pie. 'That would be impossible.'

'Come here,' said Halla, touched. She re-fastened Thora's scrunchie and fluffed her ponytail. 'I won't be gone for long.'

Soon after, Thora and Mr Walters watched Halla and Marina slip into the sea and shimmer away on the long journey towards the Sea Floor.

The sun slipped behind a high fat cloud.

'Write if you remember!' Thora shouted at the ripples on the surface.

Chapter 28

9 PM
The Loki
Kangaroo Bay
Tasmania
Antipathies

Mother has left to vote in the elections on the Sea Floor. It is an epically uplifting momentum in history for every sea creature ever invented. But the polly ticks isn't nearly as exciting as the sunshine this might shed on my disappeared father.

I do hope that Mr Walters' back is all right.

We really need to get serious about finding Cosmo's relatives. I am not sure that he is in full comprehension of why we left him alone in the boat all day yesterday. Or if he understands why he is not allowed to roam freely. Now that Mother is gone, he will descend into a navy blue, nay midnight mood if we don't pay him treasure-chests of attention. He will miss Mother. Me too.

Chapter 29

'Pong here.'

'Hello,' said Adelaide, trying to disguise her nerves. It was 8 a.m.

'I've had a complaint from one of the guests. Mr Fung Soo called me on my emergency number five minutes ago.'

'The ... the perfume maker in Room 19?' asked Adelaide.

'Perfume *magnate.* He was woken up this morning by the telephone. He had not requested a wake-up call. A very loud flatulent noise was then released into the receiver. He is furious and wants to see a doctor immediately. He thinks the noise may have ruptured his eardrum, which in turn may have an effect on his olfactory system.'

'His what?'

'His sense of smell, you stupid woman. A perfume magnate needs to be able to smell things. And I smell trouble.'

'Of course, Madame Pong.' This was the first Adelaide had heard about the incident. 'I'll sort it out. Don't you worry.'

'These guests have not come to the hotel to be woken with eardrum-exploding fart noises.'

'I know.'

'Sort it.'

Click.

Chapter 30

Mr Walters poked his head into Thora's room. 'The best cures for goodbyes,' he said, referring to Halla's departure, 'are hellos. What do you say we go and find a relative of Cosmo's to say hello to?'

Thora hopped off her bed and nodded. Cosmo regarded them both expectantly.

'I've been reading the guidebook,' continued Mr Walters. 'I think I know the best place to start looking. It's within walking distance.'

'But can your *back* last the distance?' Thora asked, concerned.

Mr Walters smiled so broadly that Thora could see the bridgework in his mouth. 'I think Sha and the girls at the hotel have cured me! Look at this!' He leaned sideways, stood straight, then leaned to the other side. 'Canadian Airforce Sidebends,' he said. 'I haven't been able to do those for years!'

'That's brilliant,' said Thora, following him into the living room.

'That's not all,' said Mr Walters, leaning forward and letting his head drop. 'I can just about touch my toes!' His fingers reached his shins. But then again, it is a long way to the floor when you are six feet and four inches. 'Bother,' he said. 'Almost! Can you?'

'I'll try,' said Thora. She reached down and with hardly any effort, flattened her palms on the floor.

'Jolly good,' clapped Mr Walters.

Thora did a handstand and held it until water started to leak from her blow hole. She hopped back on to her feet, ponytail swishing.

Mr Walters moved on to his next act: jumping jacks. Thora wondered if excitement about the Sea Shrew's death had gone to his head. The lampshades rattled and the floor shook under his feet as he scissored up and down. His hat fell off and landed directly on Cosmo's head, covering the peacock's eyes and causing him to crash into the sofa.

'Oh, Cosmo,' said Thora, trying not to laugh. 'Are you all right?'

Cosmo, besides being vain, did not have the best sense of humour in the world. He tossed the hat off and fled with a bray to Thora's bedroom.

'Hey, come back here,' shouted Thora. 'You've got to be with us on this expodiction!' Trevor's words came back to her. 'We better take care to keep your profile low!'

She took a backpack out of her closet and insisted Cosmo climb in. Mr Walters tried to help, but Cosmo's feathers were too long to fit. Cosmo endured the process with the air of a martyr.

'This won't work,' said Mr Walters, frowning. 'But the old red wagon might!'

Many years before, the family had used the wagon to wheel Halla around on the deck. But the novelty had worn off after a while and the wagon had been stored away.

A few minutes later, they set off in the direction of Blackie's Bother: Mr Walters in the lead, followed by Thora pulling the rickety wagon containing one blue peacock wrapped in a Portuguese tea towel.

A few people glanced their way, but nobody stopped them to enquire about their strange cargo.

'It's such a lovely morning,' exclaimed Mr Walters, striding through town like a Norwegian race walker.

'Wait!' said Thora, running to keep up.

For Cosmo, the journey was bumpy and a little bewildering.

Mr Walters consulted the map in the guidebook and turned down a gravel path to Boat Harbour Road. They climbed a small hill and continued along a path towards the mountain.

'A superlative view,' he said, breathing deeply. 'The light is truly astonishing!'

As they walked, something else came into view: square white buildings scattered on the distant green like dice on a green-felt billiard table.

'We've come 'round the back road to The Deep Breath Hotel!' exclaimed Thora.

'This guidebook is twelve years old,' said Mr Walters. 'It would have been published well before the hotel was built. The map indicates a bird sanctuary, "teeming with Indian-blue peafowl"!'

They hurried down the slope into the denser brush at the base of the mountain. Suddenly the crooked shack with the ghostly blue door came into view.

'Here we are!' said Mr Walters

'This can't be it,' said Thora, shaking her head.

'Oh, but it is. Most definitely.'

'But Felicity brought me here yesterday,' said Thora. 'While you were being raked and soaked! There are no peacocks here. Not a one.'

'Let's have another look,' said Mr Walters, ducking through the wind-battered door.

Thora removed the tea towel, which had become tangled in Cosmo's tail feathers. Always prone to motion sickness, Cosmo looked more green than blue as he climbed out of the wagon. They walked through the house and out the back door, into the clearing. Mr Walters was already on the far side, searching through the scrub.

Cosmo bounded off to sniff around.

Thora stood very still, watching a yellow-tailed black cockatoo land on an overhead branch. She saw a wallaby, a blue-tongue lizard, and a pair of small birds with white and black heads and cherry breasts.

But no peacocks.

'I'll be back in a minute,' Mr Walters called out. 'I want to check something in the house.'

Cosmo's sniffing had taken on a new urgency. Thora trailed after him. Felicity had called it her 'special place' and Thora could see why. It was like a secret garden for animals and birds. Further into the bush, Thora noticed a thin stream with mud banks cracked by the sun. The water source would offer relief to thirsty critters. If it ever got around to raining, that is. She wondered if Felicity had ever seen a peacock in the sanctuary, and she made a note to herself to ask.

Eventually, Mr Walters returned carrying a notebook with a rusty coil binding. 'How very, utterly, implausibly *weird*.'

'What is it?' asked Thora.

'The Visitors' Book.' He showed her. 'These entries date back almost twenty years, when the sanctuary was established. They all mention peacocks.' He flipped to a later section. 'Then, let me see ... about four years ago, the comments refer to wallabies, blue-tongue lizards, snakes, wind, a storm, a bush fire – nothing about peacocks. But this is the strange part. The last entry is by a wildlife expert from Germany, just last summer. Listen.' He cleared his throat and began to read: 'My uncle visited this sanctuary many years ago and said it was full of blue-necked Indian peacocks. As a wildlife officer, I am very disappointed to see the peafowl are all gone. Where are they? – Heather Graf, Potsdam.'

Chapter 31

Mr Walters was once a sports journalist for the BBC. He was good at asking questions. Yet when he asked people in town about the peacocks, nobody seemed to know. Or really care!

'Maybe they flew away!' said Gemma at Wheely's.

'Maybe they died from a virus,' said the lady at the post office.

'No great loss. Peacocks are not an indigenous species, anyway,' said the man at the petrol station.

'Peacocks are a total nuisance,' said the man at the bakery.

'Noisy, filthy and stupid!' said the baker's assistant.

'Not a promising start to our investigations,' said Mr Walters, as they returned to the *Loki*. But at the op shop he had managed to purchase a more recent edition of the guidebook: it made no mention of the sanctuary, or of the peacocks.

'It's as if they never happened,' he said. 'Be reassured, however. The truth always leaks out in the end.'

His words did little to console Thora. Parched and sweaty from their long walk, she peeled off her Hallaskin and put on her swimsuit. As she tried to pep up Cosmo with a bowl of tonic water and a sprig of rosemary that she had collected from the side of the road, Mr Walters handed her an envelope.

'What's this?'

He raised his eyebrows. 'I don't know. It was in the letter box. Open it up.'

Thora read the letter aloud:

Dear Thora,
I was wondering if you would like to come to The Deep Breath Hotel today to discuss a business arrangement. Mr Walters is welcome to come along and enjoy another session in the Aqua Solarium. Free of charge, of course.

I hope to see you soon.

Regards,

Adelaide Ferguson

P.S. When you buzz in at the front gate, tell them you are here to see me. I'll join you by the swimming pool.

'Marvellous,' said Mr Walters, clapping his hands. 'Why don't we go now!'

'Didn't you say The Deep Breath Hotel was a *silly* place?' asked Thora.

'Did I?'

'Yep.'

'I spoke too soon.'

Thora went to put on a fresh wetsuit. Cosmo lay on the end of her bed watching her every move.

'Don't fret,' she said sympathetically. 'We'll get to the bottom of all this.'

Chapter 32

It was not yet nine, and already Adelaide had been up for three and a half hours. Her hair was limp and her skirt still stained with papaya juice that her naughty daughter had 'accidentally on purpose' spilled on it.

The telephone shrilled and she picked it up.

'Pong here. What. Is. Going. On? I've had three more calls in the last hour. Mrs Cho said she was served orange juice this morning, despite making it very clear on her application that she is on a citrus-restricted diet. And another more serious one from Ms Sowloon.'

'The opera singer?' Room 9.

'She found some sort of faecal matter in her shoes.'

'Ficklematter?'

'Poo,' said Madame Pong.

'Maybe a possum slipped into the grounds ... We do claim this place to be very nature friendly.'

Madame Pong's voice would have chilled one of Bruce's gin and tonics. 'I don't care if the *Titanic* crashed into the hotel. I just don't want the guests to notice.'

'I understand.'

'And what about the ruckus in the Aqua Solarium? Mrs Ni Lent has complained that her meditation time was brutally disrupted.'

'It won't happen again,' promised Adelaide. This crowd were proving especially highly strung. The biggest pile of whingers she'd ever catered for. Just her luck.

'My gougers are ready. What about your dinosaurs?'

'You'll have them in time,' insisted Adelaide.

How, she had no absolutely idea.

'You sound in a way I don't like. I shall ring you tonight. At home.'

At the hotel's main gate, Thora pressed the intercom to announce their arrival. A buzz admitted them into the exclusive resort for the second day in a row.

They followed the path to the swimming pool, passing the kimono-clad guests with their handbags and water bottles, to the wok-shaped pool.

Sipping their drinks and lazing in the sun, the guests around the pool exuded the oily grandeur of the very rich. Perhaps this was because they *were* very rich.

Eventually, Adelaide appeared. She wore a wide grey skirt patterned with miniature white poodles. Though her face flickered with worry, and her make-up was smudged, her big hair-do remained immaculate.

'Miss Greenberg! Mr Walters! So glad you came! How is your back today? You're standing much straighter!'

She ushered them towards her.

'What a marvellous place you have here,' said Mr Walters.

'I'm glad you like it,' said Adelaide with a tight smile.

He waved at someone he had met at the Aqua Solarium the previous day and went over to speak with him. Before long, he was sitting on the deck trying to press his chest to his knees.

'Now,' Adelaide said to Thora, 'why don't we sit down over there under the umbrella. There is something I would like to ask you.'

Chapter 34

It took them quite a while to sit down because Adelaide kept having to stop and speak with the guests. While Thora waited, she noticed a large orange stain on the hem of Adelaide's skirt. Shame – it was such a pretty skirt.

Finally, Adelaide drew up a chair. 'Felicity seems to like you.'

'Really? That's nice. Where is she?' asked Thora.

'With her father.' Adelaide paused. 'Viv used to be Felicity's baby-sitter, but she can't help me this week. Tell me, have you ever worked with children?'

'Worked? No. But I've played with them heaps.'

'Would you like to earn some pocket money?'

'No, I think I've got some money in my pockets already,' said Thora, pulling out a five-dollar bill.

'I mean extra.'

'But there won't be much room. These pockets are quite small.'

Adelaide glanced at her watch and pressed her fingers to her temples. 'We've had some unexpected difficulties, Miss Greenberg. As I explained, our usual sitter is unable to help out. And Felicity has a lot of energy.'

'Please just call me Thora.'

At that moment, a mop of straw curls appeared on the pool deck wearing only a nightgown.

Adelaide looked over. 'Felicity!'

'Felicity?' said Thora.

'She should be with her father,' said Adelaide crossly. 'I simply *cannot* rely on him! Which is why I need you, Miss Greenberg.' Adelaide's smudged eyes had a desperate look. 'I've tried many other sitters, but they find her, well, let us say *hard to keep up with*.' Adelaide was babbling now, her eyes flitting between Thora and her daughter. 'She's very intelligent and gets bored easily and, well, it takes a special person. I think you have those qualities.'

Felicity had taken hold of the leaf-catcher: a long metal stick with a net at one end. She scanned the water.

'Oh, dear,' said Adelaide.

Everything happened quickly. Two chubby guests in kimonos surrounded Felicity. The taller lady produced a camera from her quilted bag and tried to take a photo of her friend posing beside Felicity.

Felicity lowered her head, stepped back.

Adelaide sprang to her feet. 'Felicity!' she cried.

Felicity looked over at her mother. The net on the leaf-catcher knocked the camera from the photographer's hand. The woman fell with a dismayed wail to retrieve it.

'Come. Over. Here. At. Once!'

Felicity spun around. This time the metal pole hit the smaller woman on the head, rather in the manner of a scene from one of the films that Thora had enjoyed watching on board the *Loki*. Felicity let go. The net landed neatly over the woman's face so that for a second she resembled a bee-keeper Thora had seen after Halla swam the Arno. The woman cursed, flailing her arms. Confused, Felicity took another step back – into the deep end of the pool. There was a small splash. Then she disappeared from view.

Adelaide's scream made everyone jump.

Chapter 35

Adelaide dashed to the edge of the pool. 'She can't swim! Lifeguard! Help!'

'She can't swim?' said Thora.

The lifeguard looked about now, dozily, and blew on his whistle.

The two women in kimonos were hopping up and down.

'Crikey, what a pile of wastrels,' said Thora, pushing her way through the crowd. Where was Mr Walters? She was amazed to see him standing stupidly by the edge with everyone else. She dived in, grabbed the girl by the shoulders and dragged her up and over to the side. 'Up you go, Miss Boasty!'

'Thank goodness!' cried Adelaide.

Felicity coughed and coughed. 'Whaddya mean "Miss Boasty"!' she spluttered.

'You said you could swim!' said Thora. 'And you can't.'

Felicity now sat on the edge of the pool, indignant and drenched. She glared at the water. 'I was only tryin' to scoop a beetle outa the water! Now he's gone! He's probably drowned!'

'*You* could have drowned,' said Thora.

The lifeguard hovered over them. 'Iseverythingallright? Iseverythingallright?'

'Everything is *fine*,' coughed Felicity.

'Naughty leettle girl,' scolded the woman in the kimono. 'My camera ruined! I will tell Madame Pong!'

The other woman nodded.

'Go away,' said Felicity rudely. 'And never take my photograph again.'

Mr Walters asked to see the camera. He wiped it down and pressed the button. A light flashed. 'It hasn't been damaged.'

'Yes, yes, it has!' insisted the woman. 'Look at the dent!'

'I'm *so* sorry, Miss Tonkin,' said Adelaide. 'But there is no need to call Madame Pong. We'll compensate you with cash.'

'Good.'

One by one the guests returned to their drinks, newspapers and stretches.

Adelaide grabbed Thora's hand. 'So you *can* spend every day with Felicity, from nine to eight, while I work? It's only for five days – until this group departs.'

'Sure,' said Thora. 'Why didn't you just ask?' She looked over at Mr Walters, who had resumed his cross-legged position beside Mr Hoo So Kan's mat. 'But first *I* have a small favour to ask.'

'Yes?'

'Forget the money. Just let Mr Walters have some more spa and raking sessions. He loved his treatment yesterday and it's really helped him.'

'Can you start right now?'

'Yes.'

Adelaide beamed. 'Then Mr Walters can do whatever he wants. The place is his. And yours.'

'Did you hear that, Mr Walters?' called Thora.

Mr Walters slowly raised his head, opened his eye and squinted at her.

'Everything is free, Mr Walters!'

'You are my *Elite Guest*,' added Adelaide. 'If you see Sha first, she can provide you with a hotel kimono. Please wear your hotel flip-flops in the treatment rooms.'

'Of course.' Mr Walters looked delighted.

Adelaide turned to Thora. 'Are you able to stay this evening and serve Felicity dinner?'

'No worries.'

'Good. I'll have someone from the kitchen send something down for tea. Something really special. Felicity, you can show Thora where things are in the kitchen. Your father will be working late. Use the plastic plates, please.' She placed a hand on each of Felicity's shoulders and in a stern tone said: 'Most importantly, stay *out of the way of the guests*. And the sprinklers. And the treatment rooms.'

'I know, I know,' said Felicity.

'No megaphone. No poos in the shoes. No high-jinks.' Adelaide looked over at Thora. 'Children are *not* allowed near the baths. There are plenty of games and toys in Felicity's room. There's a sprinkler and wading pool behind our house if you need to cool off. The important thing to remember is: *don't let Felicity out of your sight*. Not even for a minute!'

'No ma'am,' said Thora.

'I should be finished at eight. If I can't make it over to say goodnight to Felicity, I'll call.'

Before she took up her new duties, Thora insisted on explaining the plan to Mr Walters, though she was not sure he was listening. He was acting like a kid in a lolly shop.

'I'll start with the basics,' he said. 'A long bath at the Aqua Solarium. Toot-a-loo!'

Still, it was nice to see him so enthusiastic about something other than cricket!

Thora and Felicity then followed Adelaide through the pool gate. Adelaide closed it behind them and addressed her daughter.

'Just go and change out of that nightgown first, please. There are extra shorts and tops in The Laughing Giraffe Room. Wear a hat. And put on sunscreen if you play outside.' Then she leaned over and gave Felicity an emotional hug.

Finally, to both girls' relief she was off, hair flying, a slightly mad look in her eyes.

Chapter 36

With the heaviest of sighs, Bruce loaded the films and climbed into his boat.

He'd made this trip to Gun Carriage Island once a week for seven years. The trip across the bay took him twenty-five minutes in good weather. And today it might be even faster. But this was his second trip in three days. The first one to place the urgent order with Movie Man. Now to collect the crystals. He felt tired. And old.

The trip itself wasn't the problem. It was everything around it. He'd helped Adelaide prepare the hotel for Madame Pong's latest guests. He'd packed up the last crate of Squidgy Dinosaurs. And then that blooming call from Pong demanding another thousand had stuffed up his plans to relax and watch the Ashes. Instead, for two whole days, he'd been forced to be a full-time house-husband, taking care of Felicity morning to night.

With any other child he might have been able to catch some cricket while baby-sitting, but not with Felicity.

Every time he sat down, he had to leap up again. Felicity was up with the birds, badgering and tormenting the guests, provoking irate telephone calls to Adelaide and to Madame Pong. Rich people paying through their teeth seeking the ultimate in privacy and relaxation (as The Deep Breath promised) were not very tolerant of a naked cowgirl hollering into their ears through a pre-loved megaphone in the early hours of the morning.

That was not all. Felicity had stuffed Squidgy Dinosaurs into two guest beds, squashed fresh possum poo in the stilettos of a Singaporean opera singer, and blocked the spinners on the rotating sprinklers so that an unsuspecting actress was almost disrobed by a powerful jet of water.

She'd disrupted one of Sha's deluxe Reiki sessions by playing rodeo cowboy in the waiting room. She'd called the Taipei Twins 'tuna-fish fatties'. The women had filed a formal complaint, threatening to sue if they did not receive extra servings of pudding. And then there had been the streaking incident that had caused Bruce to interrupt the meditators in the Aqua Solarium. All *that* he could just about tolerate. Felicity was just a kid after all.

What Bruce couldn't stand was missing the one link left to his past – his cricket. He'd given up playing the game totally when he'd signed on with Pong and her crazy crystals. And now he was unable even to *listen* to the Ashes.

It wasn't *fair*.

The trip took only twenty minutes. Easing into the bay, Bruce's bad mood melted away. The island was a paradise in good weather; the sort of place he sometimes imagined he could happily have lived in, had life turned out differently. But the long heat spell had transformed the island into a tinder-box. By comparison, the green lawns back at the hotel gave him a spasm of guilt – they seemed unnecessarily luxurious and very artificial.

He flung the heavy hessian bag containing the films over his shoulder and trudged the quarter mile over two burning sand dunes to the derelict mutton-bird shack. He kept his eyes peeled for tiger snakes.

Movie Man, or MM as Bruce sometimes thought of the person he was about to meet, was always ready for him, as if he could hear the squeal of Bruce's approaching footsteps in the sand.

Today was no different. A bearded figure already waited under the turpentine bush, a full sack like Bruce's own in his stringy arms.

His dark brown hair was long, thick and dusty and tied back with a string he'd drawn out from one of the sacks. Despite his isolation and meagre possessions, MM always managed to look presentable, his fingernails trimmed, his hands clean, his beard neat. He wore his usual grey-white vest and baggy shorts and his feet were bare.

Bruce handed him the movies. MM handed Bruce the crystals. (Once a month, Bruce provided him with a kilo of freshly ground organic mocha java coffee as well.)

Simple.

MM then went into his shack to make their drinks on the kerosene camp stove, a gift from Bruce.

Bruce looked forward to these coffee mornings. He was not particularly curious about MM, although he envied the man's solitude. He rarely stopped to reflect on their odd arrangement, which had grown more complicated over the past few years. Always a bit of a rebel, Bruce wasn't concerned that he and his wife might be doing something illicit. (Madame Pong had forbidden them to mention her name or to tell MM what they were using the crystals for. Only Bruce and Adelaide knew the secret.)

Luckily, MM seemed to enjoy collecting the crystals. And, extraordinarily, he seemed totally unfazed by the snakes. He revealed in one of their conversations his belief that if everyone kept their own counsel, everyone could go their own way. Despite his haunted green eyes, there was a happy-go-lucky quality about the man.

They drank their coffee as they always did – sitting on a log under the crackling shade of the dying turpentine bush. In glorious silence.

Like MM, Bruce was a man of few words. Even in his cricketing days, he'd preferred to play the game, not talk about it. But that was a long time ago. So long, he could barely remember. Though he looked to be in his thirties, Bruce Ferguson felt he was approaching his first century. Which in a way he was.

Today Bruce broke the golden rule to keep the visit short. He checked his watch. The day was boiling hot and he felt lazy and rebellious. Adelaide had told him they'd found a baby-sitter, so he didn't have to get back for Felicity. And the cricket didn't start again for another few hours. He'd bring the crystals back in his own time. When it suited *him*. 'Maybe I could stay awhile and watch one of the films with you,' he said.

MM nodded. 'No problem.'

It was an old film, and Bruce felt nostalgic.

Chapter 38

In the Aqua Solarium, Mr Walters breathed in and exhaled slowly. *One-two-three.* The spa bath felt unusually warm today.

It was extraordinary how the worries of yesterday had just melted away – like the hoarfrost on the window near Vladivostock as the sun returned after an absence of four months. The *Loki* would get fixed in due time. Halla would have a lovely reconciliation on the Sea Floor with her family and friends. Cosmo would find his relatives.

Before he'd put his back out fixing the radio aerial, Mr Walters had looked at an old snapshot of himself holding hands with Imogen in Battery Point. They were so young. It had made him feel unbearably sentimental.

It was not that he wished to wrestle back the arms of the grandfather clock in his cabin. Yet for the past year Mr Walters had grown achingly aware of his advancing years. His lack of zip. His aches and pains. When he'd been ill with flu, he'd at least had a reason to feel tired. But now all he had was his age. Eighty-three years of it.

Was this feeling of well-being just a second wind? A final burst of energy before he was bowled the big one?

He removed his eye mask and climbed out of the bath. His knees did not crack. His back did not creak. His head did not reel.

He lifted his arm and pretended to throw a cricket ball. Easy. It was as if he'd been oiled from the inside!

If Imogen had been here with him now he would have twirled her around and around, until they both collapsed, dizzy and laughing, with a splash, into the spa bath.

Chapter 39

Adelaide's private phone was ringing yet again.

'Where is he?' It was Viv at the hangar, calling for Bruce. She was furious.

'Isn't he with you?'

'No, he is not.'

'Then he must be—' How Adelaide wished that she could just blurt out the truth. It would all be much easier if Viv knew about the crystals on Gun Carriage Island, but Madame Pong had issued the strictest instructions. 'He's been helping me here,' Adelaide corrected herself. 'These guests really are the most demanding we've ever had!'

'Oh, fiddlesticks,' exploded Viv. 'Here's me trying to make squidge for a thousand extra dinosaurs ... and that layabout husband of yours is a no-show. I'll bet he's been loafing again, listening to the radio.'

'Calm down. I'm sure Bruce is on his way,' said Adelaide unconvincingly. 'So you have everything you need? What about the peacock?'

'Didn't your husband tell you? Don't you two speak? I thought that's what being married was about.'

Adelaide said nothing and put down the phone.

Chapter 40

In The Laughing Giraffe Room, Felicity refused to wear the clean clothes that had been laid out for her. She chose instead the hessian sack and the dirty pair of purple shorts. She scowled when Thora pointed to the sneakers. 'Don't need 'em,' she said, shaking out a pink shower cap from the bathroom.

'What's that for?' asked Thora.

'I wanna take you on a special kind of hunt,' Felicity announced.

'How special?' asked Thora nervously. Felicity's near-drowning experience had not dampened her spirits!

'A scat hunt!'

Thora did not think she had heard correctly.

'Poo!' said Felicity. 'Last time I collected 159 poos from the lawn.'

Thora went outside and scanned the green. 'I don't see any.'

'You are not lookin' hard enough!' said Felicity, pulling the door of The Laughing Giraffe Room shut behind her. 'They're everywhere.'

'Don't the guests wonder about it?'

'They think it's organic fertiliser – or mud! But it's not! It's poo! Mainly wallaby, possum and pademelon. The occasional wombat too. An' if you're *real* lucky, a Tasmanian devil scat. I found one about a month ago with bits o' bone still in it – and a penguin feather!'

'Bone?'

'Of a small baby. The thigh bone, I reckon!'

'You're fibbing,' decided Thora.

'Them devils are small, but they got big jaws!' said Felicity. 'All the better to EAT you with!' She lunged at a passing guest and snapped her arms.

The guest waggled her finger at Felicity and hurried away.

Thora couldn't help but get drawn in to Felicity's plan. And once they'd started looking, it became clear that Felicity was not joking. There was poo everywhere! The turds were small and, despite the sprinkler system, quite dry and hard. Using their bare hands, they filled the shower cap in a few minutes.

'We've got eighty-one here!' said Felicity.

'How do the animals get in with the fence all around?' asked Thora.

'They just do,' said Felicity knowingly. 'They're real thirsty in this heat and they love to eat the grass, speshully after it's been watered. Mum's eyes aren't the best. She don't even see 'em!'

'What? The poo or the animals?'

'Both!' laughed Felicity.

Felicity then insisted that Thora follow her to the back door of one of the treatment rooms. 'You stay here!' she whispered. 'If you don't know what I'm doin', you won't get into trouble.' She tiptoed in, returning in less than a minute with a gleeful expression on her face. The shower cap was empty. 'Let's scram!' she cried.

'But where's the poo?' asked Thora.

'I dumped it in the mud bath!'

'Felicity!'

'Don't ya love the idea of the cussomers havin' a mud bath in possum and wallaby poo?'

Thora laughed. 'Did anyone see you?'

'Nope,' said Felicity, breaking into a run. 'I did it fast. Wanna see my bedroom?'

'Sure,' said Thora, quite dizzy.

The girls returned to the Fergusons' house, behind the hotel.

Felicity ran ahead while Thora stopped to remove a brown smear from the bottom of her slipper. She understood now why Felicity needed to be watched closely. And why the guests eyed the little girl so warily!

*

Inside, Thora stopped to let her eyes adjust. 'Felicity?' she called. It was not at all the sort of home where she could imagine a whirlwind like Felicity living happily.

The living room was narrow, with a mint-green carpet and cream walls with books high up on shelves. At the end sat two chairs that had the texture of oatmeal porridge, with a large wood-encased radio between them. Opposite was a beige chintz sofa sprinkled with orange cushions. There was a gas fireplace and tall brass lamps and, on one wall, a dozen gold-edged china plates commemorating the British monarchy.

The cluttered darkness made her think of the Allbent Cinema. The grand but faded furniture could have found an easy home in Snug House, the home of her English friend Louella. The mugs with pictures of King George, Queen Elizabeth, Princess Di and Crown Prince Fred and Mary reminded her of the stuffy antique stores that she had visited in Portobello Road when Mr Walters was helping her choose a Royal Doulton figurine of a balloon-seller to send her grandmother, Dottie Greenberg, on her seventy-fifth birthday.

'In here!'

The kitchen was also old-fashioned – but in need of a tidy-up. The table was a battleground of spilled orange juice, burnt toast and cereal boxes on their side.

'Daddy never cleans up,' said Felicity, following Thora's gaze. 'It makes Mummy cross but I think it's funny.'

Thora checked the fridge for the food that Adelaide had promised to send from the hotel kitchen. But there wasn't any.

'I'm glad,' said Felicity, peering in. 'The hotel food is disgusting. I hate toad food.'

'Don't you mean tofu?' asked Thora.

'That's what I said.'

'I promised your mother I'd feed you.'

'Can you make pancakes?'

'Not very well. I'm better with pineapple sea-foam birthday cakes. Or seaweed peach strudels.'

Felicity's face lit up. 'Sea-peach stoodles sound good,' she said. 'How do you make 'em?'

Thora checked the cupboards for ingredients. The Bakelite containers marked FLOUR, SUGAR, BROWN SUGAR were full, with only a few weevils, nothing serious. And the pantry contained every sort of dried noodle and canned fruit and vegetable imaginable, including peaches.

'Sea-peach stoodles, here we come,' announced Thora. 'First we'll wash our hands. We don't need possum scat in our pudding. Then we'll get this mess sorted.'

Felicity groaned, but there was a smile on her dirty face as she danced around the kitchen with the broom.

chapter 41

After they had eaten, Thora opened the windows in the living room and the two girls lay on the carpet, heads on the orange cushions, listening to an old Trini Lopez record from Bruce and Adelaide's collection. The fruity breeze felt cool on their faces. Felicity yawned and lay still. It was the first time that she'd been quiet all day long. It was also the first time that Thora had thought properly about Cosmo since she'd left the *Loki* that morning. She hoped he was safe alone

on the boat. She started to tell Felicty about her pet peacock and stopped. Though Felicity seemed to love animals, she was very tired.

'I'd like to go to the North Pole,' said Felicity, sleepily. 'I want to make snow angels. And see an icicle.'

Felicity could hear about Cosmo another time.

'Why is the hotel air-conditioned and the house not?' Thora asked.

'Mum and Dad can't get used to it. I'm so boiled.'

'You could always take a cool bath,' said Thora.

'They spend hours in the bath upstairs,' said Felicity. 'Every single sloliptary day.'

'We could add some ice cubes to the tub. It would be fun.'

'Not allowed in the special bath.'

'Why "special"?'

'The magic crystals keep them young,' Felicity yawned. 'Nobody's allowed in there. 'Cept them. Madame Pong says.'

'Who's that?'

'My godmother. But I know where the key is.'

'Where?'

'Mum's pet purry.' She yawned. 'Shhhh!'

'What is a pet purry?'

But Felicity was already asleep. Thora turned on her back and clasped her hands behind her head. Magic crystals! Now she'd heard everything. With her outlandish stories and strange way of speaking, Felicity well and truly reminded Thora of her younger self. Except that Felicity had a father.

With a sigh, Thora turned on her side, cupping her face in her hand. Her eyes ran over the antique radio, the porridgy chairs, the dusty plates and mugs. To live next door to a hotel and an ultra-modern health spa and still hold on to this ugly furniture was weird. Maybe the stuff had belonged to Felicity's grandparents and they didn't want to throw it out.

Thora got up, put the cushions away and turned off the record player. Then she carried the sleeping girl up the stairs. They had been so busy in the kitchen that they'd never made it to her bedroom.

She lay Felicity fully dressed on the bed, covered her with a sheet and looked around.

The room was small, and smelled of burnt cinnamon. Despite the pale blue walls and fluffy white carpet, it was an urchin's room – which is to say it was very Felicity. On the floor were piles of bottle caps, lolly wrappers, seagull feathers, fossils, shells, a desiccated dragon-lizard and even a mound of dead beetles. On the dresser, there was the 'pre-loved' megaphone (minus the batteries), a heart-shaped clock that buzzed and a wind-up pug dog. The only picture on the wall was a framed photograph of an odd woman with red chopsticks sticking out of her bun. She was dressed in a grey pantsuit and held a rat-like dog with bulging eyes and a smushed-in face.

Written in the bottom right-hand corner was: 'To Felicity Ferguson. From your godmother, Madame Pong.'

The image of the dog and its owner made Thora, once again, think of Cosmo's dejected expression as he watched her prepare to leave for the hotel. 'Please let him be there when I get back,' she whispered. 'Don't let the peacocks – I mean beetles – bite,' she said, turning off the light.

Before heading back downstairs, Thora paused in the hallway and swallowed hard. Despite the bottles of water she'd drunk, her throat was dry, her legs prickly, her blow hole funny. Maybe she should dampen down. Adelaide wouldn't be back for another half hour, by which time Thora would be completely parched.

And she wouldn't mind having a look at the crystal bath that Felicity had mentioned.

To be safe, Thora listened for the sound of approaching feet, but she could hear only grasshoppers and the creaks of an old house adjusting to the cooler temperature outside. Tiptoeing in her windsurf slippers, she opened the door at the end of the hall. Bruce and Adelaide's bedroom.

Inside were twin beds with scotty-dog bedspreads and matching bedside tables.

She crossed the thick white carpet. Where would Adelaide have hidden the key? Felicity had said it was in the pet purry, whatever that was. There were over a dozen little containers on the dresser. And three old-fashioned glass bottles of Blue Waltz perfume. Thora couldn't resist. She lifted one up and pinched the little

rubber pump. A puff of scent reached her nostrils and she made a face: it smelled of rotten lilies. She waved her hands to disperse it and continued her search.

Then on the third shelf of a cupboard beside the bathroom door, Thora noticed a silver bowl. She reached up and lifted it down. There was no lid and small bits rained down on her. Dried flowers and petals smelling strongly of roses and cloves.

Potpourri.

Smiling, Thora found the key in amongst the dead leaves.

She unlocked the door and turned on the light. The room sprang to life with a thousand bulbs. The effect was so glaring that she had to close her eyes for a second. When she opened them again, she saw that the bathtub was larger than a regular tub. It shone with what looked like clusters of diamonds, but was smooth to the touch.

She turned on the water and without removing her wetsuit, stepped in, splashing herself all over. Almost immediately, she began to feel queasy. The lights made everything shimmer, as they had in the Aqua Solarium. Around her neck the projectionist's ring was warm and humming, like the clock on Felicity's dresser.

Looking up, she suddenly noticed a row of wigs on the bathroom shelf – an army of big, starchy white-blonde hairdos, just like Adelaide's hair. She counted seven. They were mounted on Styrofoam heads that stared down from the shelves with vacant eyes. They followed her like the round windows at the front of the marshmallow hotel.

So this was why Adelaide's hair never moved!

Thora had thought that Adelaide just used lots of hairspray. But now she saw that her hair was plain fake. She climbed out of the bath and touched one. It felt like the nylon hair on Holly's Barbie doll.

Thora towelled herself quickly and backed out of the room, pulling the door closed. As she tucked the key back into the silver bowl, checking to make sure that she'd cleared away any fragments of spilt potpourri, she could hear the phone ringing downstairs.

She ran to answer it.

Chapter 42

'Pong here,' came a strange voice.

'Pong where?' answered Thora, sniffing her armpits. 'I don't smell anything.'

'Who am I speaking to, please?'

'Thora Greenberg. Who am *I* speaking to?'

'Madame Pong.'

'Felicity's godmother!' cried Thora.

'Where is Adelaide?'

'She's not here now,' said Thora. 'But she will be here soon. Are you the owner of The Deep Breath Hotel who lives in Asia somewhere?'

There was a long pause in which Thora could hear the short sharp barks of a dog in the background.

'Taipei.'

'The home of the tuna-fish fatties!' said Thora.

'The Taipei Twins own the best restaurant in the city. My dog is a VIP diner.'

'I hope he's not a vee-eye-pee dinner.'

'I will try Adelaide at the office,' said Madame Pong.

There was a *click*.

'Hello? Are you there?' Thora put the phone down. 'Sense of humorous failure or what!'

The image of the wigs floated back into her mind. She did a cartwheel to dispel the queasy feeling that rose up in her as she recalled the row of Styrofoam heads. She scanned the bookshelves for something to read, to take her mind off the bathroom, and took down a copy of a book titled *What Katy Did*.

She opened it up. There was an inscription in faded blue ink. 'For Adelaide on her sixth birthday: October 1, 1944. Love Mummy and Daddy.' It was a very old book, published in 1887. Thora flipped through the sea-scented pages. 'This Adelaide must be Adelaide's mother,' she said aloud.

Chapter 43

An hour later, Adelaide found Thora curled up on the chair below the plate commemorating the wedding of Mary to Crown Prince Fred.

'What are you reading?' she demanded.

'An antique book,' answered Thora, leaping up. She noticed that Adelaide's hair looked a little crooked on her head. 'Have you read it?' she asked nervously. 'It's about an extraordinary family of naughty children in the olden days. It's a field and valley of tears that their mother is not alive, but they do have some compensensations – I mean they *do* have a father, after all. *And* they have each other! It almost makes me feel a little sorryful for those of us who are lonely children. Like me and Felicity!' She was aware that she was babbling, and she felt her face grow hot.

Adelaide gave her a strange look and held out her hand. 'I'll take that now.'

'Are you a lonely child too?' continued Thora.

'Lonely child? I have no idea what you are talking about,' snapped Adelaide. 'Are you unwell?'

'Oh no, I am very well, thank you. Just a little mired in scrapes from year yesterday. The book has the atmospheric pressure of *Anne of Green Gables*, though of course that book was about a true orphan girl, wasn't it?'

'How did it go tonight?' asked Adelaide, plucking the book out of Thora's hands and placing it firmly back on the topmost shelf.

'Splendiferous,' said Thora. 'Couldn't have been brighter. I mean better!'

'Did she stay out of trouble?'

Thora decided not to mention their scat hunt. 'I think so.'

'Did anybody call?'

'Yes! The Madame from Pong!'

Adelaide looked horrified. 'You *spoke* to Madame Pong?'

'Well, I tried, but she wasn't very chatty.'

'What did she say?'

'That the tuna-fish fatties give her vee-eye-pee dinners. Or was it her dog?' Thora scratched her elbow. 'What is a vee-eye-pee anyway?'

Adelaide's face had grown white. She looked more like a Barbie doll than ever. 'Did you say anything to her? About what you were doing here?'

Thora thought of Adelaide's scotty-dog bedspreads, her perfume bottles with the plastic pumps, the pet purry, the bathroom, the creepy wig collection. 'She didn't ask,' said Thora, inching toward the door.

Adelaide's hand shook as she pointed to the vehicle that had appeared in the drive. 'I have arranged for Trevor to take you home.'

'Thanks,' said Thora. 'See you tomorrow! Early and bright!'

Adelaide scrunched her eyes at Thora, as if forcing herself to smile, and shut the door between them.

Relieved, Thora climbed into Trevor's Combi. 'Where's Mr Walters?' she asked.

'He left a while ago. He wanted to jog home,' said Trevor, switching on his headlights.

'Jog?' Thora had never known Mr Walters to jog. He had always said that he was far too tall – and lazy – to be a jogger.

Chapter 44

Cosmo was not on the boat when Thora returned to the *Loki*. She felt panicky: her worst fear confirmed.

From the deck, her eyes darted over to the rocks on the beach, up into the bushes with their snakes and scorpions, now plunged into darkness. 'Cosmo? Where are you?'

Footsteps on the pier made her spin around.

'Mr Walters!' she blurted. 'I can't find Cosmo!'

Mr Walters appeared not to hear her. He was wearing a pair of navy sweatpants and a baggy sweatshirt. Though his face was bright red and dripping with sweat, his movements were as light and airy as a rhythmic gymnast's. He stopped and kicked off a pair of enormous white leather trainers. He wore no socks. In the moonlight, Thora could see his long, rather yellow toenails.

'That's a new look,' she observed. She had never known him to cover his legs with anything but cricket whites.

'I couldn't perform the cat stretch in my trousers,' he said, without a trace of irony. 'Sha loaned me this splendid outfit! But the joggers are a tad small.'

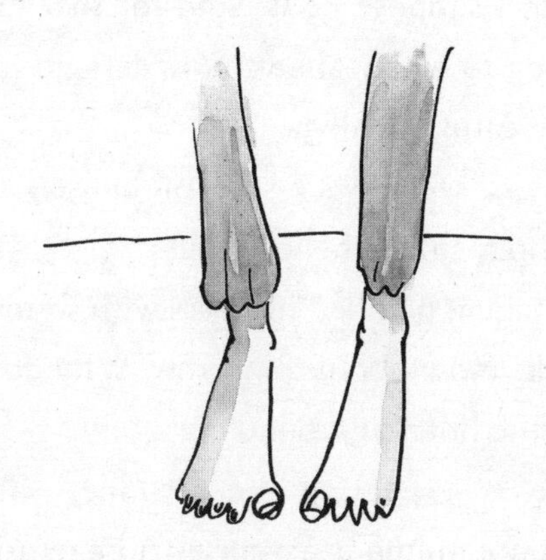

'Did you jog all the way back?'

'Yes indeedy! But I didn't let my heart rate get over 120.'

Thora could no longer stand the chit chat. She gazed at Mr Walters. 'Cosmo is gone,' she announced, loudly and clearly. 'I can't find him anywhere.'

'Really?' Mr Walters used his sleeve to wipe the sweat from his forehead and from the back of his neck. 'Maybe he's on the roof.'

'I checked. He's not.' Worry clouded her thoughts. 'I think he was disappointed about our visit to the sanctuary.'

Mr Walters waved away her concerns. 'He's a *peacock*, Thora. He doesn't understand *what* we were doing there. Anyway, he often wanders off.'

'No, he doesn't!' said Thora. 'And he might only be a peacock, but he understands more than we think. I'm sure he knows he's not welcome in town. It must hurt his feelings that people here don't like peacocks! Cosmo is a very intelligent peacock!'

'Yes, dear, I suppose he is. And for that reason, you have nothing to worry about. Now let's go inside. The mozzies are eating us alive.'

Mr Walters seemed so sure of himself that for a moment Thora almost believed him.

In the kitchen, he filled his glass with water and took a long drink. 'Now, about tomorrow. Why don't we aim to head to the hotel at around eight?'

'Adelaide is expecting me at nine,' said Thora. 'Though how can I go if Cosmo isn't here?'

'He will be,' said Mr Walters, almost irritated. 'I'll walk over with you. I'm going to begin my morning with fifty-five laps.'

'Laps of what?'

'The pool, my dear girl.'

'That's a lot of tumble-turns,' said Thora. 'Why fifty-five?'

'Because that's how old I was when I last swam a mile! And if I'm going to enter the Charity Swim, I have to practise up a little!'

Thora stared. Mr Walters was certainly bursting with new plans! And his reaction to Cosmo's absence was alarming. She decided to get right to the point: 'Mr Walters, I think something *very* strange is going on at that hotel.'

'It *is* strange,' agreed Mr Walters. 'But in rather a magnificent way!'

'They have a secret bathroom. Their spa bath is even

brighter than the baths in the Aqua Solarium! And what is even weirder is that Adelaide's hair is fake! She wears wigs!'

Mr Walters looked only mildly interested.

'Could she be bald? Like Bruce?'

'Now, now, Thora.'

'Well, could she?'

'I doubt it,' said Mr Walters. 'And besides, it's not the most unusual thing, if she was. My own hair is thinning ...'

'But you're eighty-three!'

'Yes, and I don't feel a day over thirty!' Mr Walters declared. 'Especially after my first mud bath. Very invigorating!'

Thora's breath caught in her throat as she recalled Felicity's scat collection. 'You had a *mud* bath?'

'It didn't smell particularly ... *fragrant*. But the mud cleanses the pores and renews the skin remarkably well. Now, I'd love to hear your musings. But not tonight, if you don't mind. I can feel my hamstrings tightening up and I need to do a few stretches.' He opened the fridge. 'Also, we're going to have to stock up with proper food from now on. The nutritionist at The Deep Breath said my diet is appalling. No more meat pies, I'm afraid!'

'But you love them!'

'Not any more. Too many trans-fats,' he said. 'Goodnight!'

Chapter 45

When Mr Walters had gone to bed, Thora took another look around for Cosmo. She searched the deck and checked the roof. She even looked in the cupboards and drawers. 'Something is royally rotten in the state of Tasmania,' she declared, glaring in the direction of Mr Walters' closed cabin door.

Back in her own cabin, Thora changed into her pyjamas and reached for her journal. But her thoughts were circling too fast to write them down. First. Cosmo was missing and Mr Walters didn't seem to care. Only this morning, Mr Walters was asking around town about the sanctuary. And now he was so full of himself and his soaks, mud baths, stretches, laps, diet and hamstrings that he had no time to worry or even wonder about Cosmo's disappearance.

Thora scratched her leg with her pen, recalling Mr Walters' jumping jacks. Yes, she ought to be happy about his extra energy. And she had been so this morning when she watched him try to touch his toes.

But she wasn't happy any more. The Charity Swim troubled her. Not once while Halla had swum the lakes and rivers of the world had Mr Walters expressed a desire to swim. Mr Walters' new athletic personality was unnatural and extreme. The twinkle was gone from his eyes. It was as if her wise, sensible, slow-moving Guardian Angle had been kidnapped by the very sharks that her mother had gone to the Sea Floor to vote against. And in his place they had sent up to earth a reasonable facsimile: a man who, by all accounts, approximated Mr Walters but was not Mr Walters at all.

They'd pilfered his essence!

She flicked bits of the clove-smelling potpourri off her ponytail, and put her journal away. It was no use.

She couldn't think straight. There were too many questions.

Where *was* Cosmo, anyway?

She closed her eyes.

In her heart was a huge emptiness the size of Mr Walters, Halla and Cosmo combined.

She felt very alone.

Chapter 46

Peace was descending on the grounds of The Deep Breath Hotel as the guests turned in for the night. Soon they would all be snoring as contentedly as Felicity. Adelaide, however, was pacing her living room, waiting for Madame Pong's call.

How was she going to explain the baby-sitter?

She hoped Thora had not been too ... Thora-like. 'Dream on,' she said, recalling Thora's report about the VIP dinners.

To calm herself, Adelaide sat down on the floor and crossed her legs. The stain on her skirt came into view.

It struck her that no matter how hard she tried to be a perfect mother, wife, hostess and dinosaur maker, there was always a juice stain lurking on the edges of things.

She closed her eyes, trying to empty her mind of everything that had gone wrong that day. She tried to forget all the guests and their rich-people problems. The Taipei Twins' indigestion. Compensation for the dented camera after the incident at the pool. (She'd almost told Miss Tonkin to buzz off and eat a crystal.) She tried to put away all the worries she had about the baby-sitter. About what Madame Pong might say.

Adelaide did not feel any better when the phone rang.

'Pong here. Who was that girl I spoke to?'

'The new baby-sitter?' said Adelaide carefully.

'Sack her. I don't like her.'

'I can't sack her,' said Adelaide. 'I need her.'

'The child was your decision.'

'But this is your *goddaughter* we're talking about. I need help with her while I'm running the business.'

'Tell your problems to someone who cares,' said Madame Pong. 'Now, are the dinosaurs ready?'

'We still have three more days!'

'More like two. When the boat leaves in three days those dinosaurs will be on board, or no wages.'

Chapter 47

Madame Pong slammed down the receiver. The noise echoed through her clean, uncluttered room.

She sat cross-legged on her futon, glaring at the phone. She was thinking about that fateful meeting with the Fergusons at Salamanca Market seven years ago.

That was after Ting had swallowed the crystal. After Madame Pong had met Movie Man on Gun Carriage Island.

Bruce and Adelaide had been sipping tea with trembling hands at the table next to her. She'd mistaken them for driftwood sculptures, fashionable at that time in the art galleries in Taiwan. But they were not driftwood. They were an elderly couple who had once run a toy shop. The man had been a famous sportsman who'd played some tedious long-lasting Western game. The woman was a traditional Australian wife who had helped her husband with their business. Nothing special. The biggest sadness in their life was their

childlessness. Adelaide's green-tea coloured eyes had spilled with tears as she told Madame Pong – a total stranger – about how they had decided to delay children until Bruce had retired from cricket, only to discover they had waited too long. Her confession had sealed their fate. Forever.

Madame Pong scratched the thinning hair on the back of Yin-Teng. Her nails dug into his flesh. He yelped.

She hoped she had not made a mistake.

Not until four in the morning did Bruce drive home from the hangar. All night he had been making squidge and pouring the moulds with Viv. He had now to insert the crystals into the eye sockets, catch up on some sleep and then return to the hangar to begin the process all over again. He was tired and feeling sorry for himself. Viv had ticked him off for being late, and yet he could not explain the reason. He wasn't allowed to tell her about the crystals. He didn't want to tell her about the film he had watched. At least there had been the radio to listen to in the laboratory. Listening to cricket always calmed him down.

The sun had not yet risen in the sky, but the humid air promised a change in weather. He parked and went inside. The house was silent: both Adelaide and Felicity were sound asleep. He unlocked the basement door and began unloading the ten crates of Squidgy Dinosaurs. He carried them down the stairs, set them on the floor, and went back outside to fetch the crystals from their hiding spot under the passenger seat. As soon as he drew the large hessian sack into his arms he felt better: less cranky, more alert, able to face the finicky task ahead. He carried the sack downstairs and poured its glittering contents on to the table. He drew up a chair, located the rubber cement, and had managed to attach one of the eyes when his stomach gave a loud rumble. Still holding the other eye in his left hand, he climbed the stairs to make himself a peanut-butter sandwich.

Chapter 48

Thora felt she had only just fallen asleep, when Mr Walters popped his head into her cabin. 'Wake up, sleepy head!' In fact she had slept a solid ten hours. Thora sat up, rubbing her eyes. The events of the day before all surged back: Adelaide's scary wigs, the crystal-lined bath, the strange chat with Madame Pong.

Her missing peacock.

She rushed into the kitchen. 'Is Cosmo back yet?'

'Haven't seen him,' said Mr Walters, squeezing lemon into a steaming cup.

'He *never* disappears like this,' she said, opening the door to search the deck. 'I'm so worried about him, Mr Walters.'

'Yes, I can see that. Would you like a hot water and lemon? It might make you feel better. It is supposed to get your system moving in the morning.' He took a sip. 'Actually, it's rather refreshing!'

But Thora was already outside. 'Cos-mo!'

He was not on the roof. Nor was there any sign of him on the pier, on the beach or on the rocks.

She returned to the kitchen, gobbled a slice of toast, and checked the time.

Mr Walters was waiting for her, his yellow toenails poking out of the hotel flip-flops, his gym bag packed, his tinted goggles perched on his head, ready for action.

Thora didn't want to leave. 'What if Cosmo returns while we're away? He'll think we don't care about him.'

'Maybe he's conducting his own search for his relatives,' chirped Mr Walters. 'As you said, he's an intelligent bird.'

'Aren't you going to help me find him?'

'He'll be *fine*, Thora,' said Mr Walters, striding out ahead. 'Tiddily dum, tiddly dum. I say, did I tell you I was entering the Charity Swim?'

'You mentioned it,' said Thora, warily.

'Any chance you could sponsor me?'

Chapter 49

At the hotel, Mr Walters used the card that Adelaide had given him to buzz them in and they quickly parted ways: Mr Walters to the pool, Thora to Felicity's house.

Felicity bounded down the stairs to greet her. She wore the same hessian sack and purple shorts from the day before, but her face was clean, and her hair tied in neat pigtails.

'Mum's left for work. Dad's in the bath. Whaddya wanna do today?'

Thora was glad to miss Adelaide. She looked up on the topmost bookshelf. *What Katy Did* was still there, a reminder of the previous night's awkward encounter.

Thora cut right to it: 'I have a pet peacock, Felicity, and he's missing. I need to find him. Will you help me?'

'*You* have a pet peacock?'

'I do. His name is Cosmo.'

'He's missing?'

'I haven't seen him for going on twenty-four hours. He didn't come home last night.'

'That's terrible!' said Felicity.

Thora nodded. 'Have you ever seen peacocks around here? Or anywhere on the island?'

'I haven't,' said Felicity scratching her nose thoughtfully. 'But I think I remember Mum talking about peacocks.'

'And?'

'And nothing. It was ages ago.'

'Did you know that your "secret place" is a sanctuary where dozens of peacocks used to live?'

'You're jokin'?' Felicity exclaimed.

'No.'

'Well they ain't there now,' said Felicity.

'I know,' said Thora, impatient. 'I've returned there with Mr Walters, looking. Back yesterday when he cared.'

Felicity smiled suddenly. 'Did you check the lagoon?'

'Is there a lagoon?' said Thora. 'I saw a stream – but it was bone dry.'

'You have to follow the stream inaways,' Felicity said, nodding. 'The birds all go there when it's hot.'

The girls decided to take a picnic to the lagoon. In the kitchen they filled water bottles and then searched the fridge. 'No bean sprouts are allowed!' warned Felicity.

'Or tofu!' agreed Thora.

'Or lentil salad!'

Thora closed the fridge. 'Not much to choose then,' she said.

'Here's some fruit,' said Felicity. ''Cept it's well rotten.' Tiny flies swirled over the bowl.

Felicity held up three bananas. They were soft and flecked black, like a leopard. The nectarines were erupting in mouldy spots and the apples were bruised and wrinkled.

'We could still eat them,' said Thora. (Her mother forbade her to waste food.) 'We just have to cut off the rotten bits.'

Felicity located a half loaf of knobbly brown bread.

Laid out on the bench, it was not the most delicious-looking picnic the girls had ever seen.

Thora shrugged. 'It's better than nothing. The fruit might taste better *en plein air* when we're really hungry.'

But what to carry the picnic in? They searched the shelves and cupboards. Thora opened the pantry and stepped inside.

The shelves were messy but on the floor at the back, behind a bag of potatoes sprouting green shoots, sat a wicker hamper filled with purple onions.

'I've found our picnic basket!' said Thora, holding it up.

'That old thing?' said Felicity, peering in.

'Nothing wrong with "old",' said Thora, dumping the onions into an empty mop bucket. The hamper was perfect: lined with felt tartan and ratty enough that they wouldn't have to worry about damaging it. As she hauled it out, she stepped on something soft and mushy.

'Yuck!' she cried, leaning over to check her slipper. She was relieved that it was not a huntsman spider,

as she'd expected, but rather, a partially eaten sandwich. Surprisingly, there was a small, glittering stone, half embedded in the squashed bread. A bead or something. 'Hey, look at this!' she cried, picking it out.

'I smell peanut butter,' said Felicity, stepping towards her and taking hold of the hamper.

Before Thora could show her, the stone fell into the hamper and disappeared inside the dark lining.

'Somebody's lunch,' said Thora, holding up the mangled sandwich. 'I stepped on it!'

Felicity made a face. 'That'll be Daddy's. He's not very tidy.'

'Where *is* your dad?' asked Thora.

'Sleepin' by now,' said Felicity. 'He's workin' late at the hangar on the extra shipment of Squidgy Dinosaurs.'

Thora took a rag and wiped her foot. 'Well, better peanut butter than scat.'

Chapter 50

Ten minutes later the girls picked their way through the spiky grass at the back of the house, in the direction of the sanctuary. At the base of the mountain trail, Felicity jogged ahead of her, shouting: 'Cosmo? Cosmo? Are you out there?'

Thora followed with the hamper bumping against her thigh, her eyes peeled for Cosmo's bright blue train.

The sand trail sloped up through tea-trees, eucalypts and she-oaks to a hard mud path bordered by stringy gums.

They took sips of water and went on calling Cosmo's name. But the bush was silent. It would soon be the hottest part of the day and nothing stirred.

Quite quickly they arrived at the familiar black cottage.

'The lagoon is over here,' said Felicity, pushing through the scrub. 'Follow me.' She led past the caked mudbanks to the thin stream reduced to a reddish trickle. They searched for tracks on the dry banks. 'The poor birds must be dying of thirst,' Felicity said. 'C'mon. We'll just follow the stream. The lagoon isn't far.'

Felicity ran ahead, quick as a devil, and Thora had to move fast to keep her in sight. Felicity might not be able to swim, but she was a natural bushie! She stopped to point out a dusty tailed swallow perching on the top of a dead tree. She despaired about the dryness of the bush: the mud along the creek was too hard to record animal prints. But she continued to call out Cosmo's name. Thora didn't bother. She knew, deep in her heart, that they would not find her peacock at the lagoon – or anywhere around here. He'd spent most of his life cooped up on a boat sailing the seas and oceans of the world!

The truth was, Cosmo had never had to survive on his own. Everything had always been provided for him: food, water, shelter, admiration – love. Suddenly, the landscape around them appeared hostile. And Cosmo was more a preener than a fighter.

It was almost lunchtime when they returned to the shack. Hoarse from calling out and over-heated, the girls took refuge inside from the sun and grabbed their water bottles.

'I'm starving,' exclaimed Felicity.

Thora opened the hamper. Then she saw something very odd indeed. She held up a banana. It was yellow and fresh, and the black streaks were gone. 'Did you switch them?' she asked.

'No,' said Felicity. 'Did you?'

'No.'

'You must have done,' insisted Thora. 'You did, didn't you?'

Glaring, Felicity stood up and slapped Thora hard on the face.

Thora was shocked. 'Why did you do that?'

'I *said* I didn't. So stop saying it.' Felicity crossed her arms. 'Did you?'

'Nope,' said Thora, all at once aware of the silliness of their squabble. A ticklish feeling took hold of her and she grinned.

They both laughed. They laughed so hard that they had to hold their stomachs. Tears ran down their cheeks. How had the fruit gone from being rotten to fresh? It was completely crazy!

'Look at this! The nectarines have lost their wrinkly bits ... And the bread.' Thora took a bite. 'Delicious,' she said, amazed. 'Just like fresh-baked!' Surreptitiously she checked the projectionist's ring. It was warm, but not overly.

Felicity grabbed a banana, snapped off the stalk and nibbled. 'Delicious!' She stood up. 'Better than any banana I've ever eaten! Mebbe the best banana in the history of Flinders Island!'

Thora reached into the hamper and felt around inside the torn lining. She had remembered something. Then her fingers encountered it. She drew out the small stone she'd extracted from the peanut-butter sandwich earlier that day.

She rubbed it on her wetsuit, removing the brown paste. The object was not a stone: it was a crystal – bright and sparkly as a diamond.

'Could this have anything to do with it?'

Felicity stopped chewing. 'What is it?'

chapter 51

Thora bit the crystal. It was very hard and slightly gritty. She held it up to the sun. 'I found it in the sandwich.'

'It looks like somethin' belonging to one of the guests,' said Felicity.

'It also looks like the crystals in the spa baths,' said Thora.

'Like the ones in the Aqua Solarium,' nodded Felicity.

'And in your parents' bath, too,' said Thora.

Felicity looked at her sharply.

Thora felt the heat creep into her face. 'After you went to sleep last night, I found the key in the *potpourri,*' she admitted. 'I went into your mum and dad's bathroom—'

'Nobody's allowed!' cried Felicity.

'The bath was covered with lights, just like you said.

Lights and' – she waved the crystal – 'little shiny things that look like this.'

Felicity took the crystal and examined it.

'*You've* been in there,' said Thora.

'Only once. I'm not supposed to know. They'd tan my hide. And yours too – if they ever caught you in there. Or in the basement. It's secret too. I've never been down there!'

'I saw the wigs.'

Abruptly, Felicity sat and hugged her knees to her chest.

Thora persisted. 'Why does your mum wear wigs?'

Felicity was silent.

'Is she bald?'

Felicity handed back the crystal and dropped her head. 'No,' came her muffled reply. 'Her hair is just – real skinny.'

'Your dad's bald,' Thora said.

'Lots of blokes are bald,' Felicity pointed out.

Thora thought of Mr Walters' thinning hair. But he was eighty-three! 'Do you have a grandmother named Adelaide?'

Felicity looked up, surprised.

'What's her name?' went on Thora.

'One of my grandmothers was called Felicity, the other was Judith. And they both died a long time ago. I never met them.'

'Do you know the book *What Katy Did?*'

Felicity nodded. 'It was Mummy's when she was a girl. She got it for her sixth birthday.'

'Are you sure?'

'Yep, 'cause she tried to read it to me two weeks ago on *my* sixth birthday.'

Until this moment, Thora had not given much thought to the age of Felicity's parents, but now the image of Adelaide's worn hands flashed in her mind – the wigs, the Doris Day clothes, the old-fashioned house – and the faded dedication to Adelaide on her sixth birthday, 1 October 1944. Thora braced herself to ask one more question. 'Felicity, have you noticed that your mum and dad are different?'

'What do you mean?'

'They don't really dress – or act – like other people, at least people these days.'

'Neither do you,' said Felicity indignantly. 'You wear a wetsuit the whole day! You talk funny. *That's* not normal.'

'Well, you have a point, I guess,' said Thora, looking down at her beloved Halla-skin. She leaned over and pulled up the material to expose a purple shin. It seemed the right thing to do.

Felicity stared. 'You have *scales!*'

'And a blow hole!' added Thora.

'A what?' said Felicity, eyes round.

Thora leaned forward and revving herself up, shot a misty spray of water right into Felicity's face, like a puff of perfume from Adelaide's bottle of Blue Waltz.

'I'm a half-mermaid,' said Thora. 'My mother has a tail, but my father's a human. I'm a mix of the two.'

In the past, whenever Thora had revealed herself, there had usually followed some sort of drama. Even so, Felicity's reaction was unexpected. Her eyes welled

with tears. 'You're a mermaid and that's definitely not normal.'

'Half,' corrected Thora.

Felicity was silent.

'Everybody has secrets, Felicity,' Thora went on. 'Parts of ourselves that we keep hidden way. My mother told me that I must always be very careful about who I reveal my mermaidness to.'

'So?'

'Not everybody handles it as well as you.'

Felicity shrugged, wiping her eyes with the back of her hands.

Thora continued. 'I've noticed that there are a lot of secrets in your house, too. Is it just the most incredible coincidence, or are your parents actually, well, there's no other way of putting it: *old*? If your mum was six years old when she got the book for her birthday in 1944, that would make her almost seventy!'

Thora did not know many seventy-year-old women, but she knew they sure didn't look like Adelaide!

'Do you remember last night?' she asked. 'You said your parents take long baths every day – that the magic crystals keep them young.'

'The baths *do* keep them young,' whispered Felicity. She studied her dirt-caked fingernails.

'How?'

'I dunno, but they do. They keep everybody young. That's why all those people come 'ere to The Deep

Breath. To look young. Even your Mr Walters has got the bug ...'

'The baths have gotten under *his* skin all right,' said Thora grimly.

'I've snooped,' said Felicity. 'An' I've heard 'em talking. They think I'm too young to know.' She took a deep breath. 'I think the crystal you found *is* the same as the ones in the tub. I think it's a magic crystal.'

'Can we check?'

'An there's stuff in the basement too.'

'What sort of "stuff"?'

'Don't know exactly,' Felicity stood up. 'Dad works down there when he doesn't know I know.'

Thora gathered up their rubbish and put it in the hamper along with the crystal. Neither of them had to say it out loud: the search for Cosmo was on hold.

Chapter 52

Back at the house, Felicity went upstairs to see if her father was there, while Thora checked the date in *What Katy Did*. She had remembered correctly.

'Dad's gone,' said Felicity, coming in.

The girls proceeded through the airless living room into the kitchen.

Fishing inside the hamper, Thora pulled out the banana skins, the nectarine pits, the apple cores. Felicity threw them away. Then in the place where she had found the crystal, Thora felt a lump. She plunged her hand through the torn seam and produced a long, gun-coloured key.

'This hamper's a regular treasure chest,' she observed.

Felicity took the key from her and turned it over in her hands.

'What do you suppose it opens?' asked Thora.

'Shh! I'm thinking!'

Then Felicity walked down the hall until she came to a door. She fitted the key into the lock.

Thora raised an eyebrow. 'Basement key, perchance?'

Felicity turned the lock. There was a *click*.

The door creaked open.

chapter 53

First, there were the dinosaurs: dozens of them lined up on the bench. But in place of the dull marble eyes Thora had seen on the dinosaurs in Wheely's Store, each one had a pair of glittering crystals.

'Holy T-Rex,' breathed Thora.

She found it hard to wrench her gaze from them. They were the same as the crystal she had discovered in

the pantry! The projectionist's ring suddenly seemed very alive against her chest.

'Come and look at this!' Felicity said, pointing to a large cupboard.

Forgetting the dinosaurs for the moment, Thora took Felicity's hand and together they opened the wide, slatted door.

'Coats,' laughed Thora, relieved. 'Just a regular cupboard.' She pushed a couple of winter jackets aside and then froze.

'What?' said Felicity.

The cupboard was a false front for another cupboard: a two-metre by two-metre museum, of sorts – dusty, but well organised, and filled with cricket memorabilia. In fact, it was a bit of a shrine to cricket.

'It's like the Members' Room at Lords,' said Thora.

Felicity stood gazing around, arms crossed.

'The MCC in London is the most famous cricket museum in the universe,' explained Thora.

'My dad was a famous cricket player,' said Felicity.

'You're kidding!' said Thora. Mr Walters would be amazed! At least – the old, cricket-loving Mr Walters.

There were batting pads, gloves, studded boots, shirts, Wisden Almanacs dating back to 1940, bats, cricket stumps, more bats, caps, trophies, ribbons and silver cups.

Felicity lifted a coat to reveal a table stacked with framed pictures. A couple of moths fluttered up from a square of dusty glass.

The first photograph showed a batsman at the crease. A silver plaque screwed on to the frame read:

BRUCE FERGUSON HITTING 207
AGAINST ENGLAND – July 1957

'That's cracking good batting!' cried Thora.

'It's Daddy!' said Felicity, pressing her finger on the face of the man in the photograph. She lifted up the next one.

The Australian Team:
1962 – at the Adelaide Botanical Gardens

Thora scanned the names. Sure enough – there in the bottom row,

MAN OF FEW WORDS: Master of the Googly,
Bruce Ferguson – 1969

'He *was* famous,' said Thora, removing a spiderweb from Felicity's pigtail. 'You ought to feel proud.'

'Maybe I am,' said Felicity.

There were many more pictures of Bruce Ferguson in his whites, Bruce Ferguson in his cap and jersey, Bruce Ferguson signing his bat. But the photograph at the bottom of the pile was different.

A laminated newspaper portrait of a bride and groom cutting their cake and smiling at each other.

Australia's 'Master of the Googly' Bruce Ferguson, 22, weds Adelaide Amabile, 21, in Melbourne – January 1, 1959

The man had a lot of dark hair and might have been anyone. But the woman definitely looked like Adelaide!

Thora studied the couple in the newspaper, until the tiny dots that made up their faces began to swirl and dissolve in a way that reminded Thora of her fudge. 'Your parents.'

At that moment, they heard a door slam upstairs.

Thora lunged for the string and turned off the light. The *click* echoed through the basement.

From up above came the welcoming sound of Mr Walters' voice. 'Thora? Felicity? Anybody home?'

Thora was about to reply and then stopped. He might not be alone.

They heard his footsteps retreat and then the front door shutting as he went back outside.

Carefully, the two girls tiptoed upstairs. Thora waited in the hallway until Felicity had returned the key to the hamper. Neither girl felt it was safe to speak until they were out of the house.

'It's got cold!' shivered Felicity.

A cool westerly wind was blowing in off the sea and the grounds were deserted. Thora checked her watch. It was past 6 p.m.! They had spent almost two hours in the basement. It only dawned on her now how easily they might have been discovered. Her thoughts raced. Had the crystal made the fruit fresh? Was it the same type of crystal as in the spa baths? Why were they switching the marbles for crystals in the dinosaur eyes? Why dinosaurs? How could Adelaide be almost seventy and have a six-year-old daughter? How could Bruce and Adelaide have been married so very long ago?

'We'll go to the hangar,' said Felicity boldly. 'And check out the dinosaur factory.'

Thora agreed that this was the missing piece in the puzzle, but still she hesitated. 'How will we get over that fence?'

'Easy,' said Felicity. 'If you go at it from the back of Wheely's store, there's a gap. I'll show you.'

Felicity had a determined expression. She looked older than her six years.

'OK,' said Thora. 'But first, we need to tell your mother something. We can't just go off.'

'She won't notice,' said Felicity with a small scowl.

Thora stopped.

'What?' shrugged Felicity. 'She's too *busy* to notice. It's the guests' last night. I can do whatever I like.'

'You can stay at the boat tonight – with me. But we must ask her first.'

'OK,' said Felicity.

'Then we'll find Mr Walters and tell him our plan.'

'Got it,' said Felicity, leading the way to the marshmallow-shaped dining hall.

Chapter 54

Neither Adelaide nor Mr Walters were in the restaurant. Felicity went off to look for her mother in the office while Thora chatted with a large woman setting the tables in the dining hall. Her name tag read SUE. The smell of garlic and onions wafted through the building.

'What's on the menu?' asked Thora, her stomach taking over for the moment.

'Spaghetti and tofu balls,' said Sue. 'High starch for the swimmers. They'll need it. It's over ten kilometres to Gun Carriage Island. And with this westerly blowing, it's going to be hard for them.'

'Swimmers?'

'Yes,' said Sue, pointing to a banner on the wall that read GOOD LUCK, CHARITY SWIMMERS. 'We're combining the guests' last supper with the Charity Swim banquet. Some of the guests are miffed about it, but stuff 'em. Holding a dinner is a nice way to show support for a local cause. It was that tall man's idea – Mr Walters. He's a real go-er! Hey! Speak of the devil!'

Thora turned.

'I was looking for you,' said Mr Walters, sauntering towards her in his borrowed blue sweatsuit.

'I was looking for you, too,' said Thora, searching his familiar, triangular eyes. There was so much to tell!

'I'll be eating here tonight,' said Mr Walters. 'You're welcome to join in! The tucker sounds delicious!' He glanced over at the menu and breathed deeply. 'Tofu balls are pure heaven. And lentils are a tremendous source of protein and energy! I'm going to "carbo-load" in order to build my reserves for tomorrow's swim.'

'Yes, I heard,' said Thora. But there was no responding twinkle in his eye to suggest that this was all a joke. No lopsided grin. 'Are you sure you're up for it? Ten kilometres is quite far. You haven't been training very long.'

'I could swim twenty kilometres, the way I feel!' said Mr Walters.

'Can I fix you a hot water and lemon?' asked Sue.

'Yes, please!' said Mr Walters. When Sue was gone, he lowered his voice: 'You know, Thora, I'm quite proud of myself. I've given up tea and coffee completely! No more caffeine for me!'

'You've given up tea? Even Russian Caravan?'

'Yep!'

This was the last straw. She hardened herself. If Mr Walters was attending the banquet, it mean that she and Felicity could sneak over to the hangar.

'I don't think I can join you tonight,' she said coldly. 'I'll see you later at the *Loki*. I need to find Cosmo.'

'Shame,' he said.

'Shame?' repeated Thora incredulously.

'But I *do* understand.'

'Well, *that's* good,' said Thora. 'Also, Felicity might stay the night. If her mother lets her.'

'Super-dooper!' said Mr Walters. 'Oh, and Thora ... after you eat, be so good as to put all your green waste in the silver cup by the sink.'

'What? In your old cricket trophy!'

'What better use can I put it to than towards saving the planet?' he asked.

The woman handed him his cup of hot water.

'Chin chin!' he said, raising his cup.

Thora collided in the doorway with Felicity.

'Let's scram,' said Felicity. She had changed into a fuzzy blue jumper and a pair of jeans. Amazingly, she had something on her feet: a pair of very new-looking Blundstone boots.

'You seem ready for action,' said Thora approvingly. 'So you spoke to your mother?'

'Sort of,' said Felicity. 'I left her a note.'

'That's not good enough,' said Thora, marching Felicity over to Adelaide's office. But when the girls got there, Adelaide was nowhere to be seen.

Sha said that Felicity's mother was busy. 'Someone – I think it was the perfume magnate – called the Health Inspector about poo in the mud baths.'

In town, the wind was blowing rubbish down the street. The shops were closed. Just a few teenagers huddled behind the telephone booth hatching mischief.

'Follow me,' hissed Felicity, darting toward the back of Wheely's.

It was not until they reached the wire fence that Thora's real doubts kicked in. The mystery with the crystals was intriguing, but was it any of her business? Adelaide might be rather old – but then Halla was a mermaid! She should be be looking for Cosmo. Wasn't that the most important thing?

A chill ran down Thora's back and legs as she followed Felicity beside the fence. She wished she'd thought the plan out a little better. She wondered if she should stop now, take Felicity home, and resume her search for her missing peacock all by herself. After all, hadn't she promised Cosmo she would get to the bottom of all of this?

Felicity spotted the gap between the ground and the fence and stopped. 'We're here.'

The area looked well-trodden, probably by wallabies and possums. They both crawled through. Felicity repositioned the wire and held her hand up for a high five. It was too late to turn back. They crept the two hundred metres or so through the tall grass towards the hangar. The wind blew against their faces, making their eyes water. The temperature had dropped at least ten degrees since they had left the hotel.

The hangar consisted of two sections: the larger domed structure visible from the road, and a smaller, windowless flat-roofed building large enough to be a garage for a small aeroplane.

They ran around behind it and crouched next to a skip filled with containers and plastic buckets.

'Did you feel that?' whispered Felicity, tilting back her head and sticking out her tongue.

Thora held out her hand. 'You're right!'

Almost immediately the rain released the musky perfume of pine and wildflowers – as well as something slightly putrid, like old fish.

Lightning suddenly streaked the sky, followed by a crack of thunder. The rain started to fall more heavily: big, cold drops that made a drumming sound on the plastic buckets in the skip.

'Here, take my hand and keep low,' said Thora. 'We'll go and get a good look at what's going on in there!'

They ran past the flat-roofed garage to a steamed-up window.

'Crikey,' said Thora.

They were looking at a vast chemical laboratory that reminded Thora of a plastics factory she had visited near Budapest after Halla swam across the Danube in thirty-five seconds flat. On an industrial-sized hotplate sat an enormous vat.

A person strode into view wearing protective goggles and an orange boiler-suit. Thora could see spikes of blackcurrant hair.

'Viv,' whispered Felicity.

Viv lifted the lid of the vat and jumped out of the way of the billowing steam. A vent on the side of the hangar suddenly hissed, and Thora and Felicity were engulfed by a chickeny-fish cloud of steam.

'That's the mutton-bird oil,' said Felicity.

'Smells awful,' said Thora.

'Dinosaur ingredients,' said Felicity. 'It won't hurt you to breathe.'

There was a movement in the corner. Bruce stood over a barrel scooping something up. He, too, was wearing an orange boiler-suit and goggles, and under the bright lights his bald head shone with perspiration. A radio was on beside him. Another loud cheer came from it.

'He's listening to the cricket!' said Thora a little wistfully.

At that moment, Bruce turned. His arms were overspilling with blue. He strode across to Viv beside the open vat and together they started tossing what he held into the steam.

The sight was shocking.

'Those are peacock feathers!' shouted Thora.

Bruce and Viv glanced toward the window, looked at each other and carried on.

Felicity yanked Thora down. 'You dolt! Whydya do that?'

They ducked and ran toward the end of the hangar.

Thora's mind was racing. 'They're using peacock feathers to make the dinosaurs,' she whispered. 'But how? Why?'

Thora recalled the bluey-green sheen of the Squidgy Dinosaur that she had seen at Wheely's. The phosphorescence of a peacock train! They must be melting the feathers in the vats. But what did they do to the peacocks after they had stolen their feathers?

Thora felt ill considering the possibilities. Was Cosmo in that vat?

The sound of the radio commentary seemed to be growing louder. Brighter lightning veined the sky. Thora braced herself for the thunder, careful not to touch the hangar's metal sides.

There was a boom. Then from inside the building came shrieks. Both girls stood very still. 'What's that?' said Felicity in a tiny voice.

Thora put her ear against the side of the building.

These were not human shrieks.

Excitement raced through her. 'Cosmo is in there!' she cried. 'And he's not alone.'

She pulled open the heavy doors.

Chapter 56

'Blow me down the dunny!' cried Felicity.

Thora covered her mouth with her hands.

The garage was filled with naked peacocks.

That is to say, peacocks that had been plucked bare – peacocks that resembled the chickens that dangled from hooks in the restaurant windows of the many seedy ports that Thora had visited in her eleven and a half years.

Thora did a quick count. There were about forty of the birds, and they were alive, but they were in a terrible state: wild-eyed, lurching, bald!

The radio echoed loud and tinny in the bleak concrete room. Enough to drive anyone mad. 'They're using it to cover up the noise, I'll bet,' said Thora. She scampered up and tugged the cord right out of the speaker.

The silence was sudden. Like an underwater dive.

The peacocks stopped shrieking and looked towards the two girls with a blend of alarm and interest.

A single low-wattage bulb hung by a cable from the ceiling. The floor was spread with filthy straw and muddy old carpet samples. The whole place was cold and damp and smelled disgusting.

Thora waded through the birds, searching for Cosmo. Without their feathers, the peacocks all looked alike. They cowered as Thora leaned toward them, studying their features.

All but one.

'Cosmo?'

There was a familiar *bonk!*

She grabbed him and hugged him. His skin was sticky. He was so small without his feathers! So white. She swallowed hard. 'You found your relatives,' she breathed.

Cosmo burrowed his head in her neck.

Together, they joined Felicity at the door.

'Look at their goosebumps. They need to get out of this cold. Can they come to our sleepover?' asked Felicity.

'My thoughts exactly,' said Thora, gently wrestling Cosmo to the floor. 'They must come home with us. To the *Loki*. We're going to have a party.'

Felicity marched to the open door, signalling the peacocks to follow. They were hesitant at first, as if they couldn't believe their luck, and then they started to tumble out, moving as quickly as their shaky legs would carry them, into the rain, the wind and the lightning.

They had been penned up for so long that many of them were wobbly on their feet. One bird slipped in a muddy patch. Another climbed on top of an oil drum and let out an exhilarated squawk.

'This is not the best place to celebrate,' Thora scolded. 'All of you come here. We're heading to my houseboat!'

Felicity looked nervously towards the lights in the windows of the hangar where her father was boiling up the last of Cosmo's feathers for dinosaur squidge.

'Forget about them for now, Felicity,' said Thora softly. 'I need all of your attention and experteasing to get these birds home.'

Chapter 57

Cosmo was first in line behind Thora. His beak was raised at an angle that restored to him, despite his nakedness, his characteristic air of nobility. He may have been bald as a coot, but he was still the same old Cosmo!

Led by Thora, with Felicity at the back, forty bald peacocks scrabbled through the wet paddock to the gap in the fence and along the back street of town. Thora felt like a kindergarten teacher trying to lead her class through Piccadilly Circus. She counted them twice and bribed them with treats. (Peacocks liked the sort of food Mr Walters now had in the fridge.) The storm had driven people indoors: Thora was pretty sure they had travelled the distance undetected.

Finally, the girls directed the peacocks down the jetty and watched, with satisfaction, as the birds climbed single file aboard the *Loki*.

Thora filled a bath with water and, while the parched animals competed to drink, her Guardian Angle suddenly appeared at the bathroom door.

'Good gracious me!' he said.

'Mr Walters!' she cried, leading him into the living room. 'Isn't it wonderful? We found Cosmo!'

'Where? I don't see him.'

Cosmo greeted Mr Walters: *caw!*

Mr Walters stepped back, his blue eyes confused.

'All the rest are his relatives! Felicity helped me to find him. Viv and Bruce were keeping them at the old hangar in the most deportational conditions. The good news is that Cosmo is alive and well and mixing with his kilt and kind.'

'Where on earth are his *feathers*?'

'They'll be heading later this afternoon for Taipei, I reckon,' said Thora.

'Taipei? What are you talking about?'

'Viv kidnapped Cosmo! And all Cosmo's relatives, too. She's been using his feathers to give the Squidgy Dinosaurs their bluey-green glimmer. '

'I beg your pardon?'

'Felicity and I have it all figured out,' said Thora. 'We don't know how the chemical reactions work exactly, but Viv has a whole lavoritory set up in the hangar. We saw her throwing feathers into her cauldron, with our very own eyes!'

'Cauldron?' smiled Mr Walters. 'My good girl, I do believe you have concocted one of your more colourful stories. I'm rather relieved that you are returning to your old ways – you were growing up too fast.'

'She's not cockted anything,' said Felicity. 'It's all true!'

'Truth is a mobile army of metaphors,' said Mr Walters, shaking his head. He lowered his voice. 'They are not the most *attractive* creatures without their plumage. Do you really think should they be *inside*? They don't look very clean. And they might have a parasite that's made their feathers fall out.'

He had not listened to a word!

With a look of distaste, he stepped over a particularly gaunt peacock and looked out of the window. 'I say, the weather has improved.'

'No, it hasn't! It's raining again!' said Thora.

'But the lightning has stopped. And the thunder. Good news for the swim!'

'You're not still thinking of *that*, are you?' asked Thora. 'In this weather? Surely, it will be cancelled!'

'You missed a tremendous feast at the hotel tonight. I brought a big container of spaghetti and tofu balls for you, girls. It's in the fridge. Help yourself. Now I'm off to bed. The starting gun goes off at seven tomorrow morning.' He bowed and left the room.

Thora gathered Cosmo into her arms.

Felicity sat on the floor. 'Mr Walters didn't seem happy to see Cosmo,' she said.

'No,' said Thora, stroking her bird hard. 'He didn't. You'd almost think he'd gone off peacocks.'

'Well, they do look pretty weird without their feathers.'

chapter 58

Thora raided the fridge and set out everything on the floor for the peacocks to help themselves. In minutes, Mr Walters' nasty-looking seeds, nuts and soya products were gone. Then she and Felicity tucked into the spaghetti and tofu balls. They were too hungry to remember that they didn't like 'toad-food'. Soon, however, the party lost its sparkle. One by one, the peacocks drifted off to sleep,

occupying every available surface: the floor, the sofa, the chairs, the kitchen table, even Thora's bed.

Felicity, too, was growing very sleepy. She sat on the sofa with a peacock in her lap. Her yellow-brown eyes were bloodshot and her hair sprang out in every direction. 'I ain't never had a sleepover before,' she said. 'I forgot to bring my pyjamas.'

'Just sleep in your clothes,' said Thora. She found a blanket and tucked her in. 'Don't let the clown fish bite.'

'More like the swordfish,' said Felicity. 'Mum and Dad are gonna tan my hide tomorrow.'

'Nobody's going to tan anything,' said Thora emphatically. 'Now get some sleep!'

Though what Bruce and Viv would do when they discovered the missing birds was anyone's guess. She sure hoped Felicity had written that note.

Outside, the storm continued. It was almost 2 a.m. but the noise of the rain and the thunder kept Thora awake. What had occurred at the hangar was so strange, so creepy. What *would* happen in the morning? How could she take Felicity back to The Deep Breath Hotel after what they had discovered? Surely it was illegal to use feathers from live birds to make toys! Should she call the police? Parks & Wildlife?

Then there was the mystery of the crystals.

Thora shut the curtains and reached into her pocket for the crystal that she and Felicity had found earlier in the hamper. She turned it over in her hands. If crystals could make fruit and bread fresh again, what would their effect be on people? Felicity had more or less said it: the crystals were the magic element in the spa baths. Thora recalled the queasy feeling she'd had in the Aqua Solarium and then again, in Bruce and Adelaide's bathroom. There must be something very powerful in the crystals – so powerful that they made Felicity's parents younger than they really were.

And look what they'd done to Mr Walters!

But something didn't add up.

How did the dinosaurs link up to the crystals? Why were they switching marbles for crystals? Were they exporting them illegally out of Australia?

Thora recalled Felicity's mention of Movie Man. Who was he? Thora wished she had asked more about him.

The wind continued to howl and the rain to beat down. She squeezed on to the couch beside Felicity and, still holding the crystal, eventually drifted into a ragged sleep.

Chapter 59

Thora woke to the sound of an impatient rapping noise. The peacocks were awake and braying. The rain was still falling. She sprang up and fell backwards on to Felicity, who opened her eyes, frightened. 'Hey! What's going on?'

The *Loki* was dancing on a swell – the sea was in turmoil. Through the window, they saw waves rise into vertical spray.

The knocking at the door grew louder. 'Let us in!' came a voice.

'It's Viv!' cried Felicity.

Thora surveyed the birds. The peacocks looked almost as panicked as they had in the hangar. She needed to hide them. 'Round 'em up,' she whispered, rolling back the Persian carpet that hid Halla's pizza-shaped hole in the floor.

'Whatchya doing?' hissed Felicity.

Thora then opened the Plexiglas cover. 'This is a mermaid flap: it's how my mum enters and exits the

boat,' she explained. 'There's space enough for all the peacocks in here.'

The birds looked dubious, but Cosmo seemed to understand Thora's intention. He herded the peacocks toward the hole and gave each of their bottoms an encouraging peck to get them to climb down.

'Open up! Felicity? Are you there?'

'Daddy!' cried Felicity.

Cosmo was last. When he had disappeared, Thora closed the hole and quickly replaced the carpet.

'Let me in, hon,' called Bruce. 'Mummy is worried about you! She got your note and wants you home. Right away!'

Thora made a flash decision. 'You go, Felicity.'

Felicity looked unsure.

'It's best.' Thora gave her a hug. 'You go home now with your father. That's where you belong. I'll deal with Viv.'

Taking a long breath, Thora opened the door a crack and the two girls went out on deck, shocked by the wildness of the wind and sea.

Viv and Bruce wore raincoats and sou'westers. They were furious.

'Where are they?' cried Viv, trying to push past Thora.

'Let's go home, Daddy,' yelled Felicity, jumping off the boat and sprinting up the jetty.

Bruce had no choice but to follow her. Viv, however, had used the distraction to barge into the cabin. Thora ran after her.

'I know you 'ave em, you little blighter,' Viv said, wiping her potato-shaped nose. 'There's evidence everywhere.'

The cabin was indeed messy with seeds and droppings.

Viv ransacked the houseboat, starting with Thora's cabin and working her way through the kitchen, the bathroom, the cupboards. 'Where are they?' she demanded. 'I can smell 'em.'

Thora was tickled by the sight of Viv dripping water all over the carpet. Little did she know that right under her feet, forty bald peacocks huddled together in miraculous silence.

Viv then clomped toward the last room.

'Stay away from there!' shouted Thora. 'That's Mr Walters' cabin. He's still asleep.'

Viv reached for the doorknob. 'He won't know. Anyway, he ain't here!' She turned the knob and entered.

Thora rushed in behind her. The room was empty. 'Where is he?'

'Charity Swim,' said Viv.

Thora panicked. 'It can't be held in this storm!'

Viv almost looked like she was enjoying herself. 'He's doin' it all the same. I saw him with my own eyes! He was setting off as we came down the jetty! Dressed in a bright green wetsuit. He looked like the jolly green giant, though a lot skinnier – maybe more a beanstalk.'

Thora ran to the window. 'Why didn't you stop him?'

'It's not my business to meddle,' sniffed Viv. 'Besides, some people hafta learn the hard way! He's a barmy Pom, all right.'

Thora had never before felt such a tidal wave of fury towards a human. As Viv checked Mr Walters' cupboard, Thora plucked the key from the cabin's inside lock, stepped out of the room, and slammed the door behind her. Then she locked the door from the outside and dropped the key into her pocket.

'You git back here, you devil!' Viv screamed, banging on the door. 'Let me outa here!'

Thora grabbed her binoculars. She stepped on to the deck and looked out at the blizzarding sea. She could not see Mr Walters, but it didn't matter. She reached into her wetsuit and touched the projectionist's ring, hot on the chain against her skin. 'I'll go after him,' she said aloud. If Mr Walters had left when Viv was arriving, he had only been swimming for fifteen minutes. There was still a chance! But first she must release the birds. Fast.

She went back inside and tugged the Persian carpet. 'You all better get off this boat!'

From the darkness, eighty eyes looked up at Thora. They didn't move.

She mustn't waste a second more.

'OK, stay if you want. But I warn you, it's going to be a bumpy ride!'

'Let me out!' came Viv's voice.

Ignoring her, Thora ran outside to unhitch the *Loki*.

There was no regularity to the waves, no rhythmic succession. Just a tumbling of creamy swells.

She started the engine.

Chapter 60

Only a month before, as they sailed to Australia, during one of his navigational lessons, Mr Walters had spoken to Thora about the powerful westerlies of the Southern Ocean.

He had used the tone of voice that he reserved only for the cataclysmic forces of nature: the fault-lines, the volcanoes, the tsunamis. 'The Roaring Forties,' he said, 'presented one of the biggest challenges to sailors between 40 and 60 degrees latitude. Sometimes they were called the Furious Fifties and the Screaming Sixties.'

Thora thought that 'The Roaring Forties' won the most poetical-ring award.

Though, as Mr Walters pointed out, there was nothing 'poetical' about the impact of this wind on sailors! 'Very cold, dense air comes off the Antarctic ice sheet and flows north, where it collides with warmer air and water to create polar cyclones that ride the Southern Ocean. Sometimes they can blow with hurricane force – up to 170 kilometres an hour. That's faster than any bowler!'

Thora tried, with little success, to forget all of this as she turned the *Loki* around in the harbour. Cosmo emerged from the cabin. Several birds followed him. 'Get back inside!' cried Thora.

Once again the birds didn't listen. One by one they filed out and assembled on the deck, the roof, the mast – wherever they could secure themselves.

Viv continued to shout, but her voice cut out completely as the *Loki* entered the open water. The boat rose and fell, and began to slam down between the larger waves.

The spray made it hard to see what was coming next. The swell carried them up, fast, and then shot the boat down again, up and down, up and down. The impact made it hard for Thora to stay balanced, much less to scan the water. How was she going to locate Mr Walters in all this?

Though concerned for their welfare, she found the presence of the bald peacocks a comfort. She was not alone.

The *Loki* tilted. A huge wave hit the bow, and water sloshed in. The boat righted, then began to rise again, faster this time, and Thora had the same feeling she'd had on her one – and only – roller-coaster ride in Space Mountain, Anaheim, California, after Halla had swum Lake Gatenby in record time.

The cold spray numbed her lips and fingers. Thora and her charges could have been in a snow-storm, on the tundra even. But the little *Loki*, with its unlikely crew, persevered. There was no time for Thora to peer through the binoculars. As they hit on a smoother course along the side of a swell, she suddenly caught a glimpse of green about half a kilometre away! At the same moment, she also felt the projectionist's ring, its familiar and comforting heat against her skin. She reached for it: an automatic gesture lasting less than a second. She shouted to Cosmo: 'I see him! Over there!'

Cosmo flapped his featherless wings.

Thora's tiny lapse in attention cost them. She judged

the next starboard swell incorrectly. The wave slammed against them, throwing Thora against the side of the boat. The peacocks skidded across the deck. Water poured in. When the boat righted, she couldn't see Mr Walters' green suit any more.

She blinked away the saltwater.

Nothing, but a huge rolling whiteness.

In all her eleven years at sea with her family aboard the *Loki*, she had never *seen* so much water. She took hold of the binoculars.

About fifty metres ahead, Mr Walters flashed into sight again. A neon-green arm, reaching up.

Not the arm of a swimmer. The arm of a human. In distress.

Thora leaped into the sea.

chapter 61

The water tumbled her around and around. The weight of it squeezed her. It was shockingly icy.

She wondered whether she would die from the cold before she even got around to drowning.

She struggled towards the surface, trying to find the path to air through the water's crushing weight. Her arms felt heavy. Her purpose dimmed. What on earth was she doing? What had she been thinking? Mr Walters was going to drown; the forty peacocks were going to drown. And now she would drown too.

A half-mermaid. Not mermaid enough to survive the Southern Ocean. But not human enough to know better.

She stopped struggling and let the swell roll her over and over. In her hand, the projectionist's ring felt solid and eternal.

'Please help,' she said to it.

And then the forces turning her stopped.

Silence filled her ears. Is this what it felt like? Mermaids couldn't drown, but maybe half-mermaids could.

Or maybe she was frozen and would sink to the Sea Floor, her mind trapped in a useless body.

And that would be that.

She extended her arm, and her stroke met no resistance. She extended her other arm. Same thing. In three strokes, she broke the surface, gasping for breath, sucking it in greedily. She felt something holding her up. When her eyes cleared, she wondered if she was hallucinating. Around her floated a life-raft of bald peacocks. She closed her eyes.

When Thora eventually woke, she saw that she was less than twenty metres from Gun Carriage Island. The sea was completely flat, mirroring a bright blue sky, cloudless as it had been the day before. The wind had stopped blowing. She could even hear the cry of a gull overhead. Beside her, the *Loki* bobbed as if nothing had occurred. The peacocks gazed at her with bright, concerned eyes.

Thora was too weak to do anything. She lay back in the water, looking up at the sky. The miracle of the sudden calm sea meant nothing to her. 'Mr Walters,' she whispered.

Her tears fell into the Southern Ocean. She was alive, but she felt dead. Soon she was weeping as hard as the rain that had fallen earlier in the day.

It was Cosmo's honk that made her lift her head.

Chapter 62

Slowly, Thora turned.

On the highest orange boulder on the rocky shore of Gun Carriage Island stood the figure of Mr Walters in his green wetsuit.

And in the water swimming toward her was Halla, her mother, her yellow hair brighter than the sun.

Thora fell back. How many minutes, hours, days had she been out? Time had stopped. She really *was* dead.

The peacocks moved aside and climbed back on the *Loki* just as Halla's golden head broke surface beside Thora.

'Mummy,' murmured Thora.

Halla stroked Thora's forehead. For a few minutes, they floated in silence. Finally, Thora righted herself within the circle of her mother's embrace and looked up at Cosmo, who now stood nobly on the roof of the *Loki*.

'I thought Mr Walters was dead,' said Thora, looking over at the beach.

'He's very much *not*,' said Halla.

'*You* saved him?' said Thora.

Halla shook her head. 'Not me alone. I had some help. From you. From Cosmo and his relatives—' she glanced up at the *Loki*. 'And from our reliable old friend.' She lifted the projectionist's ring and squinted at Thora through the tiny hole, like a monocle.

'Do you really think the ring helped?' Thora asked Halla.

Halla let go of the ring, which fell back around Thora's neck. 'Not think, darling Thora. *Know*. Now, swim ashore with me. You'll need your feet on the ground when I tell you the rest of the story.'

Together, mother and daughter swam ashore.

'When did you get back?' asked Thora. 'Did you vote? See your parents? Find out anything about ... ?' She couldn't bring herself to say the name.

'You'll like what I have to say,' promised Halla. 'But first say hello to your Guardian Angle.'

Thora walked ashore, her entire body trembling.

Mr Walters greeted her with a nod. His hair was wet and plastered against his head, his cheeks were ruddy, his eyes rimmed red from the salt water. He took her hands and squeezed them. She stared up at him. For the first time in a long while he returned her gaze. And she was relieved to see again in the depths of his eyes the sensible, laconic, cricket-playing man who had raised her.

He shook his head. 'I'm a silly old fool,' he said.

Thora's eyes pricked.

'I haven't been myself lately, have I?'

'No,' Thora said.

'It's as if I've been in an altered state,' said Mr Walters. 'But now I've woken up. That little episode in the sea knocked some sense into me. I'm a lot creakier. But clear in the head. I honestly do not know what came over me! I remember it all very clearly – but it's as if my thoughts have been shrouded in gauze! Like the *Loki* before we arrived in Flinders! I am quite sure those spa baths had something to do with it.'

'Yes,' said Thora. 'I'm sure they did.'

'And how I would *love* a cup of tea.'

'You threw it all out!'

'I didn't!'

'You did!'

He looked shocked. 'How monstrous of me.'

From the *Loki* came a raspy call for help. Everyone looked over. The boat was rocking slightly. Another yell.

'It's Viv,' said Thora.

'That nice lady from Wheely's Store?' said Mr Walters.

'Her beef snags are impeccable,' said Thora. 'But her moral standing in the peacock universe is not. I think she ought to stay right where she is. For now.'

'I am sorry to have to interrupt this reunion, folks,' said Halla. 'But we've got some business to attend to.'

'Happy to be at your surface,' said Thora, standing to attention.

Halla's voice might have been hoarse, but the words she spoke had the effect of sunlight.

Chapter 63

'The Sea Shrew left details written on sand blocks in her vault,' said Halla. 'Marina helped me locate them just an hour after Finnbogi was elected. They contained the following lines:

The gods have met
They've sipped their tea
And this is what
They said to me.

The man I banished
Before his marriage
Inhabits an island
Called Gun Carriage.

When his fiancée
Of all these years
Kisses this hermit
On each of his ears

He will like a toad
In an old fairy tale
Recover his memory,
Emerge from his jail.

'I don't understand,' said Thora.

'I don't blame you. Here's what I've learned, with the help of Marina and Finnbogi and some sleuthy mermaids: the Sea Shrew exiled your father to the farthest away place on earth that she could imagine.'

'Where? Here? On Gun Carriage?' Thora looked around.

'Yes. She wanted a place out of the ordinary. She chose an island in Australia because she knew English convicts had been sent here for crimes in the nineteenth century. 'And before she banished him, she erased his memory.'

'How?'

'I don't know. Some sort of spell.'

'Do I dare ask ... is he still alive?' Thora whispered.

Halla and Mr Walters both said it at once. 'Yes!'

Thora felt faint. 'Where is he?'

Halla raised her finger to her lips. 'This won't take long, but I want you to hear it before you see him. Yes, it was to this very island that your father came, with only the clothes he was wearing when I last saw him. He spent the first four years in an old mutton-bird shed, surviving on bush tucker and rainwater. Then, about seven years ago, he had his first visitor. A woman whose pug dog had eaten a crystal.'

Thora recalled the yap at the other end of the phone. She felt in her pocket. She held the crystal tightly.

'As you now know, this island has an abundant supply of a unique crystal. Your father,' continued Halla, 'did not see this woman again. But not long after, he was visited by a man called Bruce.'

'Felicity's father—'

'Bruce knew that your father liked movies, and he made an offer: if your father would collect crystals, Bruce would supply him with films.'

'Movie Man!' said Thora. 'My *father* is Movie Man?'

'The arrangement made everyone happy. Your father liked to sift the dunes for crystals. When he sifted, he could recall snippets from his past. Images of cinemas and water and mermaids.'

'Did he tell you this?'

Halla nodded. 'The movies "saved" him, he said. Gave him a reason to live. And they filled in bits of his missing past. He *did* grow up in the Allbent Cinema, after all! Bruce brought him coffee, which your father loves. Everyone was happy – or at least as happy as one can be with complete amnesia.'

'Didn't anyone else ever see him?' asked Thora.

'Your father thinks it was the snakes that kept people away.'

'Is it a sort of bad luck place?' said Mr Walters, looking around.

'But it's so close to Flinders,' said Thora. 'And so beautiful!'

'There are dozens and dozens of islands around here,' observed Mr Walters. 'All of them filled with snakes. And most of them beautiful.'

'I arrived here last night, in that terrible storm.' Halla looked down at her tail. 'It was rather challenging, to have to search the island in the rain, in the dark, so I planned to spend the night in the water by that boulder.' She pointed.

'Just the sort you like,' laughed Thora. 'Lots of decorating options.'

'But I was too excited to sleep. Then I smelled something and saw smoke. I dragged myself up over the dune and there was a fire burning.'

'Lightning!' asked Thora.

'As it turned out, yes. But the fire led me to your father.'

'Was he OK?'

'Yes,' Halla laughed. 'But he was more scared of me than of the flames! Can you imagine? You are watching your house burn down and you look up through the smoke and the rain to see a mermaid pulling herself towards you, and the next thing, she's trying to kiss your ears! He must have thought he was watching a really awful film, a real bargain-basement B-movie. But when I kissed him, he remembered who I was.'

'Where is he?' asked Thora impatiently.

'He's at the shed. The rain eventually put out the fire, and he managed to save his film projector and a few other things. As you can imagine, we had a lot to discuss. He made me talk through the night. He needed to know and hear everything.'

'Did you ... did you tell him about me?' asked Thora.

'Why do you think my voice is almost gone? I've been cross-examined all night! There were a lot of years to fill in! But my tail started to dry out this morning, and so he carried me to the water and went back to get his things – and to say goodbye to the home he's lived in for over a decade, all the time we've been travelling the world.'

'Can I go find him?' said Thora.

'You'll be able to follow the tracks in the wet sand quite easily. On legs, it won't take you five minutes.'

Chapter 64

Footprints led Thora up a sandy hill.

She paused at the crest. She had waited her whole life for this moment. And now that it was here, she felt a strange reluctance slowing her movements. Her mind was racing forward, but her body held back wanting to savour each step.

Less than twenty-five metres away, she stopped again to study the ruined shed that had been her father's home. The building was charred and still smouldering. The fire had caused the roof to collapse. It had blackened the wood and tilted the structure to the right. A blast of wind would send it to the ground.

She heard a person moving about inside. Then he emerged, tall and thin with a smoke-blackened face and beard, and eyes that caught the light. In an instant she recognised – in the line of his jaw, the shape of his head, the way he stopped and scratched his elbow – something absolutely familiar. He noticed her and stood still and a smile split his face.

Thora tossed the crystal into the bushes where it belonged. Then she ran towards him. 'I found you!'

The man she had waited eleven years and five months to meet looked at her through vivid green eyes and took her in his arms. 'It's you,' he said.

TAIPEI TIMES
GREEN IN The Red!

TAIPEI TIMES

GREEN IN THE RED!

Madame Pong, allegedly the richest green woman in the world, has been arrested, and her assets seized, after an international woman-hunt that led authorities to a famous restaurant, the Dai Tin Heng on Koo Yi Road, Taipei. Madame Pong was feeding her pug dog pork dumplings at the time of her arrest and showed no emotion as authorities escorted her to a waiting police car.

Madame Pong, 62, is the daughter of the late Professor Pi Pong. She inherited her father's alternative therapy spa when he died twenty years ago. The spa, specialising in the controversial practice of 'crystal therapy', rocketed to fame in Taipei seven years ago after Madame Pong patented the design for crystal-studded spa baths, which she exported for a million dollars each to rich clients around the world. Further wealth came her way when her company floated on the Taipei stock exchange Eekobeasties Inc., a toy company manufacturing Squidgy Dinosaurs made from organic ingredients.

Sold throughout Asia, the toy dinosaurs were the unwitting vehicles used by Madame Pong to import the rare crystals from Gun Carriage Island, a tiny mineral-rich island in Bass Strait, off the north-east coast of Tasmania. The crystals were placed in the eyes of the toys and later removed and handed over to Madame Pong by a team of women called the 'Gougers'. Marble eyes were inserted in their place and the popular toys then distributed to warehouses around Asia. They were sold for $20.00 each in over 5000 shops world-wide.

The crystals are said to make people young and increase their energy and stamina. Tests are being conducted on the small topaz-like gemstones at government laboratories in Sydney, London, Taipei and New York.

Crystals were not the only illicit material used to make Madame Pong's Squidgy Dinosaurs. The story took a bizarre twist when it was revealed by Flinders Island Parks & Wildlife Officer Mike Rickard Bell that peacock feathers were used to give the toys their unique blue sheen. Information about Madame Pong's activities was first reported via telephone to Parks & Wildlife by Madame Pong's goddaughter, 6-year-old Felicity Ferguson, after she and Thora

Greenberg, 11, discovered forty plucked Indian blue peacocks in a hangar on the edge of town. Police arrested Vivienne Wheely in a bedroom of the Loki, where she was locked prior to Miss Greenberg's dramatic sea search for charity swimmer Mr Jack Walters, 83.

Wheely has been charged with cruelty to animals, and the managers of Madame Pong's luxury Spa on Flinders Island, The Deep Breath Hotel, are currently being questioned.

In an unprecedented action, the hotel has been closed by local police for the foreseeable future.

Flinders Island
Gazette
viv wheely in Happier times

FLINDERS ISLAND GAZETTE

Mrs Vivienne Wheely, 68, long-term resident of Flinders Island and intrepid owner of the Wheely's Store on Centre Street, Blackie's Bother, has been released on bail after admitting forty counts of animal cruelty. She has, however, pleaded not guilty to the charge of unlawful exportation of Incredible Crystals from Gun Carriage Island, claiming 'I had no idea they were sticking crystals into the eyes of my Squidgy Dinosaurs! I thought they were filling 'em with marbles!'

Bruce and Adelaide Ferguson of The Deep Breath Hotel have been sentenced to 20 years of community service for their role in the illegal exportation company, masterminded by the Asian crystal-therapy magnate and toy distributor, Madame Priscilla (Pi) Pong of Taipei. Parks & Wildlife has issued a statement confirming that the couple, who are believed to be 69 and 71 years old respectively, have already begun converting the lavish hotel into a peacock sanctuary. The couple will continue to live in their present residence. Their light sentence is said to have enraged Wheely, but others on the island are satisfied with the punishment, believing that nobody else should be expected to care for the couple's lively six-year-old daughter, Felicity. A former employee of the Fergusons,

Reiki expert Sha Coldstream said: 'Taking care of Felicity is sentence enough.'

The surprisingly young-looking seniors said at their hearing that they were 'victims of their innocent desire for a child'. They claim to have met Madame Pong by accident in a Hobart cafe about seven years ago. Madame Pong later contacted them with 'the devil's offer'. They soaked in the crystal-encrusted baths for many hours each day, grew young and, remarkably, had a child. But in exchange for this miracle, they were required to provide the front for Madame Pong's illegal export business, using the hotel and toy factory as a cover. Adelaide Ferguson claims they have suffered numerous side effects from the crystals, ranging from alopecia (hair loss) to a constant sense of deja-vu.

The couple's community service will also require former Master of the Googly, Bruce Ferguson, to share his expert cricket skills with younger residents of Flinders Island. He will teach cricket at the local primary school and act as a cricketer-in-residence – for the term of his natural life.

The Loki
Pacific Ocean

Dear Felicity:

I hope this letter finds you surrounded by thirty-eight Indian peacocks with their full complication of feathers having grown back.

We have set sail for Grimli-By-The-Sea so that like Cosmo, we too can gather our relatives together for a humdingle of a reunion party. My father plans to run the Allbent Cinema (my grandmother is thrilled!) and my mother will lobby for a lifetime's lease on the nearby Rock (possible now because Frooty de Mare has declared bankrupture and left town). Mr Walters is ready to trade the high seas for a more sensible life of tea, cricket and newspapers. He has given up yoga and raking and sworn off baths, preferring the unmedicated method of cleaning, i.e., showers. I must say, it's invigorating to have him back on this planet.

He has not yet forgiven himself for disposing of our precious supply of Fortnum & Mason Russian Caravan in the compost bin. But one cannot blame him. How was he to know that the crystals in the spa-bath would take him on a detour though the world of alternating therapy? They say the shock of a near-death experience – combined with missing his daily soak – is what awakened him from their effects. They say the crystals have a more dramatic impact on the very small and the very old.

Thank you for your excellent flower-girling at my parents' wedding at Kangaroo Harbour Beach. My father was pleased to fit the projectionist's ring on to my mother's finger. It seemed a miracle that it suddenly fitted her after all these years – but as we both know, some mysteries are better kept. Halla sends you her deepest phosphorescence.

I was truly sorry that Parks & Wildlife had to seize The Deep Breath Hotel. But it is fitting that those beautiful grounds will not go to waste. I have always wanted to live beside a peacock sanctuary! I think the birds are much more interesting and certainly slimmer than Madame Pong's hand-pickled guests (though I expect you might sometimes miss teasing the likes of the tuna-fish fatties).

Cosmo and his pea-hen friend were sorry to leave, but your offer to visit any time made him feel better about saying goodbye. Their feathers have started to grow back. They both have a coat of peachy down now. They are sitting up on the roof as I write this, sniffing the breeze as peacocks are pronated to do. I have promised to make them some sea-peach stoodles, as you call them, when I have finished this letter.

I spoke to Trevor before we left and he was very happy about how everything turned out. He wants to tear down the hangar and turn the land over to Parks & Wildlife. I think he also wants to restore the mutton-bird shed on Gun Carriage Island.

I am glad that everyone has been so sympatico to you and your family. Your parents did, after all, get involved with Madame Pong in order to have you!

Good night!

Don't let the tiger snakes bite!

I am yours until the end of the term of your natural life and mine,

Thora Greenberg.

P.S. Mr Walters was right. The truth always leaks out on the end. I mean IN the end. XX

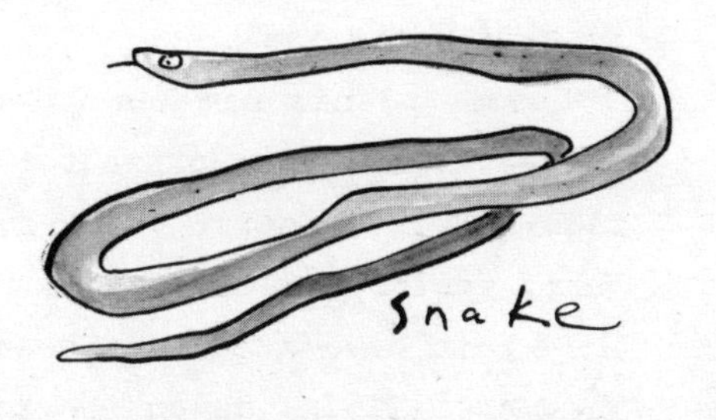

Photo © Dan Johnson

Gillian Johnson grew up in Winnipeg, where she spent her winters speed skating at Sargent Park Oval and her summers swimming in Lake Winnipeg. She now lives in England and Tasmania with her husband, writer Nicholas Shakespeare, and their two sons, Max and Benedict.

More Thora from Hodder Children's Books:

THORA

Gillian Johnson

'Ten years at sea, ten years on land ...'

It's time for Thora – half-mermaid, half-human – to leave the sea and join the rest of us on dry land. She's ten now, and the Sea Shrew's prophecy says that her days in the deep are done.

Leaving her mermaid mother and taking her pet peacock, Cosmo, Thora does her best to settle down in the seaside town of Grimli. But trouble is brewing – as it so often is when Thora's around – and she comes face to face with Frooty de Mare, a fat-cat businessman who hates mermaids.

Thora's nothing if not determined, though. She'll stop Frooty's sinister plans, whether he likes it or not ...